W9-BMM-896

VOLUME I
BOOKS 1-4

Jeanne Betancourt

SCHOLASTIC INC.

New York Toronto London Auckland Sydney
Mexico City New Delhi Hong Kong Buenos Aires

No part of this publication may be reproduced in whole or in part, or stored in a retrieval system, or transmitted in any form or by any means, electronic, mechanical, photocopying, recording, or otherwise, without written permission of the publisher. For information regarding permission, write to Scholastic Inc., Attention: Permissions Department, 557 Broadway, New York, NY 10012.

Pony Pals #1: I Want a Pony, ISBN 0-590-48583-0,
Text copyright © 1994 by Jeanne Betancourt.
Illustrations copyright © 1994 by Scholastic Inc.

Pony Pals #2: A Pony for Keeps, ISBN 0-590-48584-9,
Text copyright © 1995 by Jeanne Betancourt.
Illustrations copyright © 1995 by Scholastic Inc.

Pony Pals #3: A Pony in Trouble, ISBN 0-590-48585-7,
Text copyright © 1995 by Jeanne Betancourt.
Illustrations copyright © 1995 by Scholastic Inc.

Pony Pals #4: Give Me Back My Pony, ISBN 0-590-48586-5,
Text copyright © 1995 by Jeanne Betancourt.
Illustrations copyright © 1995 by Scholastic Inc.

All rights reserved. Published by Scholastic Inc.
SCHOLASTIC and associated logos are trademarks and/or registered trademarks of Scholastic Inc.

12 11 10 9 8 7 6 5 4 3 2 1   4 5 6 7 8 9/0

Printed in the U.S.A.   23

This edition created exclusively for Barnes & Noble, Inc.

2004 Barnes & Noble Books

ISBN 0-7607-5822-0

First compilation printing, June 2004

Contents

I Want a Pony   V

A Pony for Keeps   105

A Pony in Trouble   197

Give Me Back My Pony   295

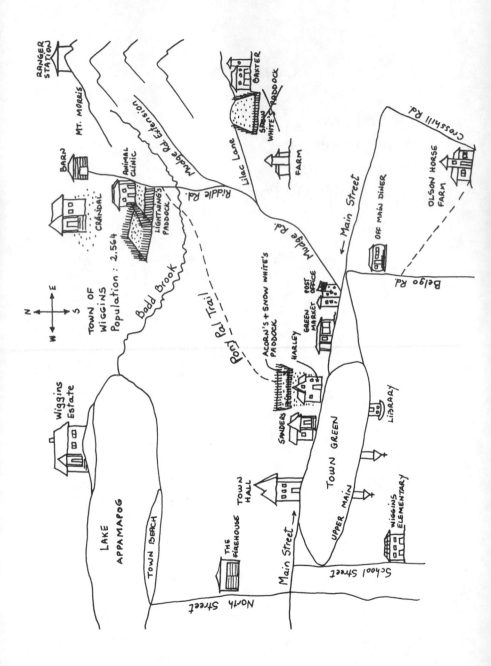

I Want a Pony

For my pal, Leslie

The author thanks Elvia Gignoux for generously sharing her lifelong knowledge and love of horses.

Thanks also to Dr. Kent Kay for medical consultation on this story.

Lulu Meets Her Neigh-bor

Lulu had been at her grandmother's for three hours and twenty-two minutes. She watched the slow-moving hands of the kitchen clock as she waited for her father to phone and say that he'd made a mistake. He'd tell her that instead of living in boring Wiggins she could go with him to the Amazon jungle in Brazil.

"Lucinda, dear. Come here, won't you?" Her grandmother was calling from the front parlor.

Lulu ran through the dining room into

the parlor. The large sunny room, facing Main Street, wasn't a regular parlor. It was a beauty parlor: *Sanders Beauty Salon.*

Grandmother Sanders was squirting a pile of silver-gray curls with hair spray. Looking at Lulu's reflection in the chrome-framed mirror she said, "Lucinda, dear, we do not run in the house. It's not ladylike."

Lulu sneezed from the irritating hair-spray fumes.

"Well, now," the pile of silver curls said, "so this is your granddaughter?"

"Yes, indeed," Grandmother said. "Mrs. Cassarra, this is Lucinda Sanders. Lucinda, this is Mrs. Cassarra."

To Lulu, Mrs. Cassarra said, "How do you do?" To Grandmother, she said, "I can't imagine suddenly having a child to raise. At our age."

"I'm only here until my dad finishes his job in Brazil," Lulu informed her. "He's raising me."

"That's right," Grandmother told Mrs. Cassarra. "And I love having my granddaughter with me. As for my age, well, I have more energy at seventy than I did when I was younger." She looked at Lulu. "Now wouldn't a cut and a permanent do wonders for Lucinda's hair?"

Even though three mirrors showed that Lulu's brown shoulder-length hair was straight and stringy, she thought her hair was just fine. She hated the idea of spending even five minutes in the stuffy, smelly beauty parlor. Now if Grandmother had pony stables, she thought, I wouldn't mind those strong odors one bit.

The phone rang.

"Would you get that, Lucinda, dear?" grandmother said.

Lulu answered the phone by saying, "Sanders Beauty Salon."

"Lulu!" the voice on the other end exclaimed. "How's my girl?"

"Dad! I was waiting for you to call. I'm going to the kitchen phone to talk."

As Lulu ran back through the dining room, she reviewed how she would plead with her father to let her go with him to the Amazon. Maybe he already realized he'd made a mistake in not taking her. Maybe he was calling to tell her that.

But Lulu's father hadn't changed his mind. "Now about your allowance," he said. "I've wired the entire amount to the bank. But, remember, it's twenty-five dollars for each week."

"Dad, there's only one diner in this town and no toy stores or anything like that. There isn't even a movie theater. What am I going to spend money on?"

"Lulu," he responded, "think of living in Wiggins as an adventure. Go exploring and study nature. We always do that when we hit a new place."

"Grandma's too strict. She won't let me do anything. I know it," Lulu said.

"I survived her," he laughed.

"Yeah, but you're a boy. She's going to expect me to do all these girl things."

Her father's final words on the subject were, "Lulu, you're a strong, independent girl. You'll be okay. Listen, they've started boarding my plane to Brazil, so let's say good-bye. I know you'll have a great time in Wiggins. I love you."

"Bye, Dad. I love you, too," Lulu said, and hung up the phone.

As Lulu got into bed that night she thought about her father. She missed him very much. And she felt lonely for her mother who had died when Lulu was four.

Trying not to be sad, Lulu thought about her past two years in England with her father. Two afternoons a week, rain or shine, she attended a riding school where she took lessons on a Welsh pony named Ginger. On Ginger, Lulu had learned to walk, trot, canter, gallop, and jump. She became such a good rider that she and her friend Emily were allowed to take the school's ponies on long trails through the English countryside.

Lulu fell asleep picturing Ginger's sprightly trot, her laughing eyes, and the proud sound of her neigh.

A few hours later Lulu woke from a deep sleep with a start. Why was she hearing the sound of pony hooves on stone, and a pony's whinny? I must have been dreaming about Ginger, she thought. But as Lulu sat up in bed and rubbed her eyes to wake herself more, she heard her grandmother shouting, "Catch that horse! Get it before it destroys everything in my garden."

"He jumped the fence, Mrs. Sanders," a man's voice shouted. "But we'll catch him. Don't you worry."

Lulu ran to the window. Grandmother's yard was brightly lit by the outdoor lights. Lulu looked down at a scene of wild confusion. A man in red pajamas, a woman in a yellow bathrobe, and a curly blonde-haired girl in a pink nightgown were all scurrying around the yard trying to catch a shaggy brown pony.

To avoid his pursuers the pony was running across grandmother's stone patio.

The girl shouted, "Stop, Acorn. Please, stop."

A big clay pot of geraniums crashed to pieces on the patio. As the pony stopped to sample the geraniums, Lulu rushed out of her room and down the back stairs.

By the time Lulu reached the backyard the geranium-munching pony had been caught by the girl. Lulu thought the girl looked about ten years old, just like her. The girl was talking softly to the pony as she slipped a halter on him.

The girl led the pony to Grandmother and stopped in front of her. "I'm really sorry," she said. "I'll make it up to you."

"How can you, Miss Harley?" Grandmother asked angrily. "These are the last blooms of the season. Now they're ruined. There must be a law about keeping a horse in the backyard."

"Acorn's not a horse, ma'am," the girl said proudly. "He's a pony." She led Acorn onto the driveway.

Lulu wanted so much to talk to the girl and ask her about her pony. But with Grandmother so angry, Lulu knew it

wasn't the right moment to meet the neighbors.

Later, for the second time that night, Lulu fell asleep thinking about a pony. This time she thought of the bold and confident little Shetland pony who lived next door. Acorn, she told herself, I'm glad to have you as a neighbor. Tomorrow I'll pay you a visit.

Lulu Gets Caught

One look at the backyard the next morning and Lulu knew that the Shetland pony's midnight visit hadn't been a dream. She got dressed and went down the back stairs to the kitchen.

Her grandmother was already at work in the beauty parlor. Lulu made herself a bowl of cereal with slices of banana. Then she went into the backyard to clean up the mess that the pony had made. Lulu figured that if Grandmother's yard looked neat, she wouldn't be so angry at the neighbors.

First, Lulu picked up the pieces of broken clay pots. While she worked she snuck looks at the Harley backyard. She was hoping to see Acorn. But all she saw was a big vegetable garden and a three-sided shed with some bikes and a lawn mower. As far as she could tell there wasn't any place to keep a pony at the Harleys'.

Then she heard Acorn's whinny. She realized that the Harleys' yard was deeper than her grandmother's. The enclosed area that was Acorn's paddock was separated from the Harley vegetable garden by a row of bushes. Lulu ran to the far end of Grandmother's yard. There, between the shrubs and the fence, she had a good view of Acorn, his paddock, and a wooden shelter.

When the small pony saw Lulu, he stopped in his tracks and stared at her. Lulu held up one of the mangled red geraniums and called his name. Acorn's shaggy black mane bounced around his head as he ran up to the fence. He was coming at such a fast pace that Lulu was

11

afraid he'd jump like he had the night before. But the pony, seeing that the geranium was held out on his side of the fence, came to an abrupt halt. In a swift, bold motion he grabbed hold of the flower with his mouth and pulled it out of Lulu's opened hand.

"You are so cute," Lulu said. Then, remembering that Shetlands can be proud creatures, she added, "You're more than cute, Acorn, you're really handsome." She stroked his cheek. He nuzzled her shoulder. Then he turned and ran off across his paddock. In the middle of the field, the pony turned and bobbed his head at Lulu, as if to say, "Aren't you coming?"

Lulu heard the Harleys' back screen door rattle shut. A girl's voice called out, "Acorn. Acorn."

Quickly Lulu squatted out of sight behind the shrub. From this hiding place she watched the Harley girl walk across the paddock toward her pony. Acorn, rather than running over to the girl, trotted in the other direction. "Come and get me," he seemed to be saying as he bounded around the field.

For a while the girl played along with Acorn's game of tag. After a few minutes and an apple bribe, the girl had a halter on Acorn and was leading him to his shelter. There she brushed him and checked his hooves. Lulu knew this meant that the girl would soon be saddling him up for a ride.

Lulu watched as the girl put a bridle on Acorn, placed a saddle on his back, tightened the girth, and pulled down the stirrups. Finally, the girl led Acorn toward a gate at the far corner of the paddock. She opened the gate and then mounted her pony. Oh, how Lulu longed to be mounting a pony herself!

When she saw that the girl and Acorn were riding into the woods beyond the paddock, Lulu decided to trail them.

In a flash she hopped the fence and ran behind the row of maple trees edging the paddock. But by the time Lulu ran through the gate, Acorn and his rider were out of sight. Lulu saw that the only place they could have gone was on a narrow trail that snaked into a dense woods.

Lulu wasn't afraid of woods or forests. She'd been on lots of nature expeditions and camping trips with her father. And trailing animals was just the sort of thing she and her father did all the time. It was one of the things he'd be doing this year in the Amazon jungle.

After what Lulu estimated to be a mile on the trail, the woods opened onto a large sun-drenched field. Acorn stopped and the girl dismounted.

Lulu hid behind a big pine tree. She heard the girl say, "Here we are, Acorn. Look, there's Lightning. She's coming over to say hi."

Acorn whinnied and another pony whinnied in return. After a quick peek to see if the coast was clear, Lulu darted to a bush at the edge of the field. From there she saw a beautiful chestnut pony that was quite

14

bigger than Acorn. The pony was galloping across the field to meet a tall dark-haired girl and a dog who had just entered the paddock.

"Hi, Anna! Hi, Acorn!" the taller girl called. "What a great day!"

"It might be great for you," Anna replied in a discouraged voice.

When the other girl and her pony reached Anna she asked, "What's wrong? Is Acorn okay?"

"Pam, he jumped out of his paddock again last night. And that mean woman next door yelled and yelled like Acorn was some wicked animal. My mom and dad are really mad at me."

As Pam gave her pony loving pats on the neck, Lulu thought about how lucky Anna and Pam were to have their own ponies and a private trail to connect their two houses and paddocks. She was daydreaming about riding a pony on that beautiful woodland trail herself when she saw that the dog was running toward her hiding bush. He barked at the bush.

"What is it, Woolie?" Pam shouted.

"Shush, Woolie," Lulu whispered.

But Woolie barked even louder.

"I think he's found something," Lulu heard Pam tell Anna. "Let's go see what it is."

In an instant Lulu considered her options. She could jump up and say, "Hi, I'm Lulu Sanders. Just thought I'd introduce myself." Or, she could make a run for it.

She made a run for it.

"Hey," she heard Anna shout, "that's the girl staying next door."

"Why are you spying on us?" Pam yelled.

Lulu reached the trail and kept running.

Back in Grandmother's kitchen, Lulu walked in circles to slow down her breathing and keep her legs from cramping. She felt like such a jerk. Now, if she saw those girls it would be so embarrassing. And in a town the size of Wiggins she was bound to bump into them sooner or later. Especially since one of them lived next door. And they probably both went to Wiggins Elementary School. They might be in the fifth-grade class that she'd be joining on Monday. I'm the new girl in school, Lulu thought, and I've made a total fool of myself before I've even met anybody.

Well, she decided, at least I won't see Anna and Pam this afternoon — because I'm going on a hike.

Lulu put a sandwich, a canteen filled with water, three cookies, an apple, and two carrots into her backpack. She folded a piece of paper, found a pencil stub, and stuck those in the pocket of her jeans.

Before going into the beauty parlor to tell Grandmother that she was going on a picnic and hike, Lulu remembered to brush her hair and pull it neatly back with a barrette.

Grandmother was in the middle of giving a pretty red-haired woman a permanent. When Lulu told her that she was going on a hike, Grandmother looked alarmed.

"Dad and I always go for hikes when we get to a new place, Grandma. It helps us get our bearings."

"Well, stick to the roads," Grandmother said. "And make a map as you go so you'll be sure to find your way back."

"Of course," Lulu said. "Dad taught me that, too."

"Indeed," Grandmother said. "And who do you think taught him?"

Lulu smiled at the thought of her father as a little boy in Wiggins.

A Pony in Trouble

Lulu headed east down Main Street. After passing two blocks of shops and houses she came to a corner where Main Street met Mudge Road. She leaned against a tree and began her map by drawing and labeling lines for the streets. Then she walked on Mudge Road.

Soon Lulu came to another intersection. To her right she saw rolling hills of squared-off fields in different shades of green and brown. Some were dotted with black-and-white cows. The only buildings she could see were a white farmhouse and two red barns on the nearest hill.

A winding dirt road led into this landscape. A faded wooden sign told Lulu it was called Lilac Lane. After Lulu added Lilac Lane to her map, she took a deep breath of the crisp fall air and headed down the road.

As she walked along, Lulu found herself thinking what a great road Lilac Lane would be for riding a pony. After about a half mile the road took a sharp turn. Lulu figured she would come upon another farm and more cows. But when she turned the corner, there was only one animal in the squared-off field beyond the bushes — a white pony. She couldn't believe her eyes.

"Pony!" she called excitedly. "Look at you. You're so beautiful."

The pony was munching grass at the far end of the field. Hearing Lulu's voice, the pony looked up. Lulu walked over to the barbed-wire fence and called out, "Come here, let me get a better look at you. I bet that you're a Welsh pony."

Lulu noticed a yellow house next to the paddock. She decided that was where the pony's owner lived. But right now there were no cars in the driveway or any other signs that the people were home.

Lulu saw that the pony was still watching her. She reached into her backpack, took out an apple, and held it up for the pony to see. "I have a treat for you," she said. That was all the encouragement the pony needed. The pony ran across the paddock in a direct line to where Lulu stood.

"You know what," Lulu told the pony. "I think this is the perfect spot for my picnic."

The pony gently pushed at Lulu's shoulder with its nose, as if to say, "Where's that apple?"

Lulu was worried that the pony would get hurt on the barbed wire. To encourage the pony to move away from the fence, Lulu reached over it and offered the apple in her open hand. The pony gently took the apple with her teeth, then backed away to savor the juicy treat.

Lulu dropped her backpack into the paddock. She carefully raised the top barbedwire strands, making just enough space to climb through into the field.

As Lulu stood up in the paddock, she saw that the pony had already eaten the apple and was now snorting around at her backpack. Lulu rubbed the smooth white slant of the pony's neck to get her attention.

"Hey, pony," she said, "I've got some more treats for you — but unless you can work a zipper you'd better let me do the unpacking."

Lulu looked into the pony's face. "You're a sweet thing," she said. "But look at all those burrs sticking in your mane. After lunch I'll pull them out. If I had a brush, I'd give that white coat of yours a good grooming, too."

The pony's ears pointed straight up to the blue sky, and her big brown eyes looked right at Lulu. The pony seemed to be saying, "I was really lonely. It's so nice to have company. Now, what's in that feed bag of yours?"

While Lulu ate her sandwich and cookies she fed the pony a carrot. Then she poured water from the canteen into her cupped hand so the pony could have at least a few licks of water. The pony's tongue felt smooth as velvet on her hand.

After lunch, Lulu took the annoying burrs out of the pony's mane. She kept the pony still by singing. "Most ponies would have to be tied for this job," she told the pony. "But you're so smart and sweet that you're staying still."

By the time Lulu picked out the last burr, she'd sung every song she knew the words to, including a few Christmas songs. The pony seemed to like "Jingle Bells" best.

That night, while brushing her teeth, Lulu looked out the bathroom window at the yards below. Wiggins was lit by the white glow of a full moon. From this second-story window Lulu had a bird's-eye view of Acorn's paddock. She could see that the Harleys had added an extension to the paddock fence. And there was Acorn looking up at it. He shook his mane, stomped his hooves, and snorted as if to say, "How could you guys ruin all my fun? I'll find another way out of this paddock. You wait and see."

Lulu heard the Harleys' back door close. She watched Anna, again in her long pink nightgown, run around the vegetable garden and through the gate into Acorn's paddock.

The little pony gaily ran over to her. After Anna gave Acorn a treat, she put her arms around his neck and hugged him.

Lulu's heart skipped a beat. "Anna and Acorn," she said wistfully to herself, "how I wish you were my friends."

The next morning Lulu went into the beauty parlor. "Grandma," she said, "I'm going for another hike. Okay?"

"Don't forget your hair appointment with

me at four o'clock," Grandmother reminded her.

"Four o'clock," Lulu echoed. She noticed a wide, flat hairbrush lying on the counter. "This is a nice brush," she said as she rubbed the stiff bristles over the palm of her hand.

"If you like it you can have it," Grandmother said. "Getting free beauty products is one of the advantages of having a grandmother who's a hairdresser."

Lulu wrapped her arms around Grandmother's waist and gave her a big hug. "Thanks, Grandma," she said. "Thank you so much."

Lulu put the brush in her backpack. Today, she thought, I'm going to brush that pony's coat until it shines.

It was another sunny day, but a little cooler than the day before. Lulu was glad that she had put a sweatshirt on over her T-shirt.

She jogged along Mudge Road. As she turned onto Lilac Lane and passed the first farm, her heart started pounding with excitement. She couldn't wait to see the white pony.

But when Lulu turned the corner in the road she didn't see the pony. She walked up to the fence. Still no pony. Had the owner taken the pony for a ride? Or had the pony only been visiting for the day? Her heart sank.

As Lulu turned to walk away, she heard a desperate, weak whinny. Looking toward the sound, she saw the white pony half hidden by a bush. The pony was lying in a far corner of the paddock and struggling to get up. Something was terribly wrong. The pony was in trouble.

A Dangerous Trap

Lulu tossed her backpack into the paddock, crawled under the fence and ran to the pony.

As she got closer she saw that the pony's white coat was covered with red cuts. Then she noticed a large bloody wound on the pony's front left leg. Lulu saw that a strand of rusty barbed wire was wrapped around the leg. One end of the wire was still attached to the post. The pony was trapped.

Lulu could see that the pony had gotten jabbed by the barbs. But even worse, each time the pony pulled to free herself, the wire around her leg would tighten and cut deeper into the flesh.

I don't care if I get cut, too, Lulu thought. I'm going to free this pony. But what could she do? One end of the barbed wire was stapled securely to the fence post. The rest was embedded in the pony's flesh. She knew she shouldn't try to untangle the pony. Not without help.

Lulu figured out that she needed a pair of wire clippers. And the pony needed a veterinarian.

The pony started to struggle again. Lulu said, "Easy, pony. Easy. That's a good pony." With Lulu's encouragement, the pony calmed down and stopped trying to get up.

Lulu realized that if she went for help, the pony would start moving again. Then that piece of rusty wire would cut deeper into the wounded leg. She decided to stay with the pony and wait for help to come to them.

She rubbed the pony's neck. Yesterday the pony's brown eyes had glowed with merriment. Today they were wide with pain and fear. They seemed to be saying, "I'm in pain and I'm afraid. Please help me."

To keep the pony calm, Lulu sang the way she had the day before.

When she saw how much the pony was sweating she fed it half of her water. Though Lulu was thirsty, too, she took only the tiniest sip to keep her voice going. She saved the rest for the pony.

Flies were buzzing around the wounds and landing on the pony. "Shoo, flies," Lulu said. She took out her map and used it to fan them away.

The sun moved across the sky.

Clip-clop. Clip-clop. Lulu heard the sound of horses' hooves on the dirt road. In the distance, she saw two people on horses. She pulled off her sweatshirt. As she waved it over her head she saw that the riders were Anna and Pam. And the two horses were their ponies — Acorn and Lightning. Lulu continued to wave her sweatshirt flag. She thought, I don't care if they think I was weird to follow Anna and Acorn yesterday. I have to get them to help this pony.

Pam yelled to Anna, "Hey, someone's signaling for help. Look."

"It's that girl from yesterday," Anna shouted.

Startled by the voices, the wounded pony began to struggle again. "Oh, pony, please don't move," Lulu said. "Everything's going to be all right."

Hearing Lulu's voice again, the pony calmed down. With one hand Lulu rubbed the pony's neck to keep her from moving. With the other hand she signaled the approaching riders to be quiet. The girls must have noticed Lulu's *shush* signal because they stopped shouting.

While Anna stayed with their ponies, Pam crawled through the fence and walked silently across the field toward Lulu and the white pony.

Lulu continued talking to the pony in a calm voice. "Pony, someone's coming to help you. If Pam can hear what I'm saying she shouldn't come any closer."

Pam stopped where she was.

Lulu continued, "Pam sees that you are caught in a piece of nasty barbed wire. We don't want to startle you because when you move the wire hurts you more. I hope she can find some wire clippers so we can cut the barbed wire. Also, she should get a vet to come as quickly as possible. I'll stay here with you, pony, until help comes."

Pam nodded solemnly at Lulu to let her know that she understood. Without a word she turned and walked out of the field. Lulu could see her talking quietly with Anna. Then the girls mounted their ponies and rode off.

Since help was on the way, Lulu decided to give the pony the rest of her water. As the pony lapped the water from her hands "Everything's going to be all right," Lulu said.

It wasn't long before Lulu saw a truck with a horse trailer bumping along the road. Pam, Anna, and a man got out of the car. Lulu was glad to see that the man was carrying a medical bag. The girls stayed at the fence while the man crawled under the fence and walked across the paddock. Lulu was glad that Anna and Pam understood that the pony might be more frightened by having a lot of people standing around.

When the man reached Lulu he whispered, "I'm Dr. Crandal, Pam's father."

Lulu said, "I'm Lulu Sanders."

Then Dr. Crandal spoke to the pony as calmly and kindly as Lulu had. "Well, pony," he said, "what kind of trouble have you gotten yourself into?"

"It's not the pony's fault," Lulu said. "The barbed-wire fence was broken."

"So I see," Dr. Crandal said. "This pony is badly hurt." While he cut the end of the wire that was still attached to the fence, the doctor asked Lulu, "Is this your pony?"

"No," Lulu said, "I was just visiting her."

All the time the doctor treated the pony, Lulu continued stroking her neck and humming softly to keep the wounded pony still.

"Well," Dr. Crandal said, "this animal certainly trusts you. Why don't you keep doing what you're doing while I administer first aid. Just move over so you can jump out of the way if she kicks."

Dr. Crandal gave the pony two shots. "One's a painkiller," he explained to Lulu. "The other is to anesthetize the area of the wound."

When he was sure the pony wouldn't feel any pain, the doctor used a pair of medical pliers to unwrap the barbed wire encircling the leg.

Then he poured antiseptic on the wound and wrapped the leg below the knee with a thick gauze bandage.

Last, he put antiseptic on the smaller cuts. "Most of these cuts need stitches," he said. "But I'm more concerned about this leg."

He looked toward the small stable that

stood in the corner of the field closest to the yellow house. "Let's get Pam and Anna over here," he said, "and see if we can't get our patient on her feet and into her stable."

After Lulu introduced herself to Anna and Pam, she explained that she was living with her grandmother. Then she said, "Pam, thank you for getting the doctor. I mean your father. I mean your father the doctor."

Pam smiled at Lulu. "I'm glad Anna and I came this way today," she said.

Dr. Crandal pulled a halter and lead rope from his medical bag. "Put this halter on the pony, Lulu," he said. "Let's see if she can stand up."

As Lulu gently placed the halter over the pony's pink nose, she tried not to think of what would happen if the pony couldn't stand. She knew that horses with broken legs were shot.

"Okay, Lulu, ask her to get up," Dr. Crandal said.

Lulu stood in front of the pony, saying,

"Come on, pony. Stand up. You can do it."

The pony tried. And tried. On the third try, teetering and tottering, she struggled awkwardly to her feet. Anna, Pam, and Lulu exchanged happy smiles. But Dr. Crandal remained serious. "Let's see if she'll walk," he said.

"Come on, pony," Lulu said. She looked back over her shoulder. The pony moved in a slow unsteady gait, putting almost no weight on the wounded leg.

Pam and Anna ran ahead to check out the stable. Lulu and the doctor moved across the field at the pony's slow, crippled pace. When they finally got the pony to the stable, Pam and Anna met them at the door.

"We changed the straw. What a mess," Pam said.

"The water bucket was filthy," Anna said. "We had to wash it out before we put in the fresh water."

Pam told her father, "I think this pony's

been neglected. You should say something to her owner."

"I've got more important things to talk to the owner about," Dr. Crandal said. He explained that the pony needed more than the emergency care he'd given her. "But I can't do X rays and treat her," he said, "before I talk to the owner."

"You keep saying, 'the owner,' Dad," Pam said. "Don't you know who it is?"

"I've never treated this pony," he said. "Some new folks moved into this place a while back. I've been trying to remember their names."

"It says 'Baxter' on the mailbox," Pam said.

"Good for you, honey," Dr. Crandal said. "That's it. I've noticed this pony when I've driven by. I figured I'd hear from the Baxters sooner or later." He gave the pony a kindly pat. "Poor animal, I didn't expect to meet you this way."

The three girls remained silent as Dr.

Crandal thought about what to do. "I remember hearing that the Baxters are in real estate. They bought Ritter Real Estate. You girls stay with the pony while I take a run over there."

Lulu followed Dr. Crandal out of the stable. "Dr. Crandal," she asked, "if the Baxters don't want to spend the money to have their pony treated, could they just, you know . . ." She couldn't finish the question.

Dr. Crandal finished it for her. "Have it put to sleep?"

She nodded.

"I know that sounds terrible to you, Lulu, but the pony belongs to its owners. It's their property. So it's their decision whether the pony receives treatment."

Lulu nodded again. She felt Dr. Crandal's hand on her shoulder.

He shook his head and said, "But to be honest with you, at this point I don't even know if the pony can be saved."

Lulu's Reward

When Lulu came back into the pony's stall, Anna was telling Pam, "I've got to go now. I promised my mother I'd be home by five to help her with a party at the diner."

"You're coming to my house tonight, right?" Pam asked.

"Yes, my mom said she'd drop me off," Anna said. "Are you sure it's okay for Acorn to stay, too?"

"Sure," Pam answered.

Lulu looked at her watch. It was already four-thirty. "Anna, when you get home could you tell my grandmother why I'm not home?"

"Sure," Anna said. She frowned. "Your grandmother really doesn't like ponies, does she?"

"I guess not," Lulu mumbled. "She's not much of an outdoor person."

"But you like ponies," Anna said.

"I love them," Lulu said. She combed her fingers through the injured pony's mane. "Especially this one."

"I hope the pony is okay," Anna said as she left the stable.

A few minutes later, Pam pointed over the wall separating the pony's stall from the storage area. "Look Lulu," she said excitedly. "There are a bunch of award ribbons."

Lulu scratched the pony's forelock, "Good for you, pony," she said. "You're a winner."

Pam went into the storage area and climbed on a bale of hay to get a closer look at the ribbons. "Wow," she exclaimed. "Lots

of them are first place. And there's a blanket in here with her name on it."

"What is it?" Lulu asked.

" 'Snow White,' " Pam read.

At the sound of her name Snow White turned her head toward Pam and whinnied, as if to say, "That's it. That's my name."

"Snow White," Lulu repeated. She looked into the pony's eyes. "What a perfect name for you. Well, Snow White, it's a pleasure to meet you." Lulu could tell by the look in Snow White's eyes that she liked hearing her name.

When Pam came back to the stall side of the stable, Lulu asked her, "Do you see a lot of injured horses at your father's animal clinic?"

"All the time," Pam said. "I help out. Especially when we have injured animals boarding in our stables."

There was a moment of silence.

"Do you think Snow White will get better?" Lulu asked.

Pam said yes and tried to smile, but Lulu saw tears in her eys. Pam turned from Lulu and walked to the doorway. "I'll stand here," she said, "so I can see if the Baxters come."

While they waited, Pam asked Lulu questions about where she came from and why she was in Wiggins. She wanted to know all about her riding lessons in England.

Lulu learned some things about Pam, too. She found out that her brother and sister were five-year-old twins namod Jack and Jill. And that she had had her own ponies since she was five. Lightning was her second pony.

Both girls heard the car coming down the dirt road. "The car turned into the driveway," Pam said. "It must be Mr. Baxter. I'll go tell him what happened."

"Don't forget the part about how brave and wonderful Snow White has been," Lulu said.

"I'm also going to tell him how great you've been," Pam said. "You're a hero. You should have a reward."

While Pam was gone, Lulu daydreamed that Snow White would be cured of all her injuries. And that the owner would be so grateful that he would give her Snow White as a reward. She was imagining her first ride on Snow White when her daydream was interrupted by a harsh, angry voice.

"What have you done to my daughter's pony?" a man's voice bellowed. A big bulk of a man stood in the stable doorway.

Snow White snorted.

Lulu stood up and said, "Nothing. She was caught in barbed wire. I waited for help."

Just then Dr. Crandal walked into the stable. Lulu sighed with relief. Maybe he could get this horrid man to stop yelling. He was upsetting Snow White.

Dr. Crandal introduced himself.

"I'm Brook Baxter. What's going on here?" the man said.

Dr. Crandal explained that the pony's leg was seriously injured. "I won't know if it can be treated until I've taken X rays. And even if it's a wound that can be stitched, we won't know for a week or so if the leg has responded to the treatment."

"If it can be treated and she recovers, what kind of shape is she going to be in?" Mr. Baxter asked.

"I can't tell you if she'll completely recover the use of that leg," Dr. Crandal answered, "anymore than I can predict if I can save your pony. The tendon —"

Mr. Baxter interrupted Dr. Crandal. "What you're saying is I could spend a lot of money on an animal that could be useless or have to be put down."

"Yes," Dr. Crandal said. "That's what I'm saying."

Mr. Baxter turned to Lulu and yelled, "It's all your fault, young lady. Trespassing on private property and getting that dumb animal to run where she had no business running."

47

"She's not dumb," Lulu protested, "and I — "

Mr. Baxter cut off Lulu by turning to Dr. Crandal. "Just put the creature out of its misery," he said. Then he pointed at Lulu. "And I hold this girl responsible."

"Mr. Baxter, just what is it that you hold Lucinda responsible for?" a woman's voice asked.

Everyone, including Snow White, was startled by the loud voice. They all looked to the door to see Mrs. Sanders standing in the doorway.

Before Mr. Baxter could answer, Grandmother was telling Lulu, "Come to me, child." Then she ordered in her sternest voice, "All of you, come out here. I want an explanation for what is going on."

Who's Going to Pay?

Pam stayed in the stable with Snow White while Lulu, Dr. Crandal, Mr. Baxter, and Grandmother Sanders gathered outside. Even though Lulu was dirty, Grandmother put a protective arm around her shoulder.

Mr. Baxter and Grandmother glared at one another. "Do I know you?" he asked.

"I know you," she answered. "I'm your wife's new hairdresser. I did your daughter Rema's hair, too. How dare you take that tone with my grandchild? Now what is going on here? You'd better be straight with me."

Lulu was amazed that Grandmother was taking her side without even asking her what happened.

When Mr. Baxter began his accusation that Lulu had trespassed on his property and that it was her fault that the pony was injured, Dr. Crandal interrupted.

"Mrs. Sanders," Dr. Crandal said, "your granddaughter did the right thing. She found a pony in trouble and she stayed with the animal until someone came along to help." The doctor turned to Mr. Baxter, "You should be thanking Lulu, Mr. Baxter, not accusing her."

"Thank her for what?" Mr. Baxter said. "That my pony has to be put down?"

Lulu spoke up. "But Snow White doesn't have to be put down. I'll pay for the medical bills. I have a bank account."

"Lucinda," Grandmother said, "that's your allowance for the year."

"Everyone calm down," Dr. Crandal said.

50

"Snow White is Mr. Baxter's pony. The medical bills will be sent to him."

Having her grandmother's arm around her shoulder gave Lulu courage. "What about your daughter?" she asked. "She must love her pony."

"Rema's in boarding school. I wanted to sell the pony before she left," Mr. Baxter snapped.

"She probably wants her pony to be here when she comes home for vacation," Lulu said.

As if to plead her own case, Snow White whinnied from the stable.

Mr. Baxter fell silent for a second. Then he turned all his attention to Lulu. "I'll tell you what," he said. "I'll pay the medical bills. But if she has to be put down, you'll pay me back for my expenses."

"It's a deal," Lulu said. She extended her hand to shake on it. Mr. Baxter didn't move. "I said it's a deal," Lulu repeated. Mr. Baxter finally shook her hand.

"So it's settled," Dr. Crandal said. "Let's

get Snow White over to my animal clinic. We've wasted enough time."

Mr. Baxter looked at his watch. "I'm late for an appointment to show a property. Call me tonight, Dr. Crandal, and let me know what's up." He turned and stomped out of the stable.

"Come along now, Lucinda," Grandmother said.

Lulu looked up into her grandmother's stern face and asked, "Please, can I lead Snow White into the trailer? She might be scared."

Grandmother sighed. "I'll wait in the car. But be quick. We have bingo tonight." Lulu knew better than to ask her grandmother if she could go with Snow White to the animal clinic.

Once Snow White was safely inside the trailer, Lulu put her cheek against her neck. "Bye, Snow White," she whispered. "Good luck."

"I'll call you as soon as my dad tells me

how Snow White is doing, okay?" Pam said.

"Okay," Lulu said. "Thanks."

As Grandmother and Lulu drove down Lilac Lane behind the trailer, tears came rolling down Lulu's cheeks. "Snow White might die," she said. "Maybe her leg can't be fixed."

"You'll just have to wait and see, Lucinda," Grandmother said. "You've done everything you could."

Lulu remembered something that she should tell her grandmother right away. "Thank you, Grandma," she said, "for defending me with Mr. Baxter. I know you don't like horses."

"I may not like horses, my dear," Grandmother said, "but I think a great deal of you. It was clear that you had put yourself out to help a living creature. What you did for that horse was just the sort of thing your father would have done. Your mother, too, for that matter. I'm proud of you."

Now Grandmother had tears in her eyes, too.

But by the time Lulu and Grandmother got back to the house on Main Street, Grandmother was back to being her old fussy self. "Now take off those filthy shoes and clothes, Lucinda, before you step on the carpet. Bring them right down to the laundry room, sneakers and all. And for goodness sakes, take a shower and wash that hair. And put on a dress."

Half an hour later Lulu was starting down the back stairs, clean and in her good dress. The phone rang. Lulu ran down the stairs into the kitchen. But Grandmother had already answered the phone and was saying, "Well, thank you so much, Mrs. Crandal. It's very thoughtful of you. But Lucinda is going to bingo tonight. Perhaps she could come for a sleepover another time."

Lulu fell to her knees at Grandmother's feet and clasped her hands in a begging position.

Grandmother looked at her in horror and signaled her to get up. While Grandmother chatted on with Mrs. Crandal about what a huge success the bingo games had been as a church fund-raiser, Lulu scribbled a note.

It's hard to make friends in a new place. Please, please can I go? Pam's a very nice girl.

She put the note in front of Grandmother. Grandmother read it, then studied Lulu with a level serious gaze and told Mrs. Crandal that Lulu could go to the sleepover.

After Grandmother hung up, Lulu showered her with kisses and thank-yous.

"Well, good gracious, child," Grandmother said.

As Lulu was changing back into jeans and packing her overnight bag, she wasn't only thinking about her new friend, Pam. She was thinking about her new pony friend, Snow White.

Half an hour later the Crandals picked

up Lulu. Mrs. Crandal was driving. Pam and the twins sat in the backseats. Lulu got in next to Pam. Before she could ask, Pam said, "My father's still working on Snow White. We don't know any more about her condition."

Lulu held back from asking if she'd be able to visit Snow White in the animal clinic.

The Crandals' house was spacious and comfortable. Lulu especially liked the large kitchen with a big couch in the corner and a round oak table in the middle of the room.

Mrs. Crandal went right to the stove to finish cooking dinner. Lulu and Pam set the table.

A few minutes later Lulu faced a plate heaped high with steaming spaghetti. Just as she was about to lift a big forkful to her mouth, Dr. Crandal came in.

Lulu's heart started to pound. Her hunger disappeared. She put her fork down.

"Well," Dr. Crandal said. "Glad to see you here, Lulu. It'll save me a phone call."

"How's Snow White?" Lulu managed to ask.

"I was able to stitch her up," he said. "If the barbed wire had dug in another quarter of an inch I wouldn't have been able to repair the leg. Your keeping her still the way you did saved her life."

Everyone at the table clapped.

When they'd quieted down, Lulu asked Dr. Crandal, "Will she be able to carry a rider and jump again?"

"We won't know that for a couple of weeks," Dr. Crandal answered. "It depends on how well she recovers. She'll need a lot of care."

"We'll take care of her," Pam said. She looked at Lulu, "Won't we?"

"Yes," Lulu said. "Yes, we will." She stood up. "Could I go see her right now?"

"Sit down and eat your dinner and let the pony rest. She's all drugged-up right now anyway," Dr. Crandal said.

Lulu sat back down. Pam leaned over and whispered in her ear. "When I invited you to a sleepover, I didn't say where we were going to sleep."

"Where?" Lulu whispered back.

Pam whispered to Lulu, "In the barn. With Snow White."

Lulu had no trouble having two big helpings of spaghetti and a bunch of the best chocolate cookies she'd ever eaten.

Snow White's Sleepover

After they did the dishes, Lulu and Pam headed out to the barn with their sleeping bags. The full harvest moon glowed on the horizon.

"Look, the moon is so bright you can see the yellow and orange leaves on the sugar maple tree," Pam said.

Lulu liked that Pam noticed things like that. "That's just the sort of thing my dad says," Lulu giggled.

The girls passed the horse paddock.

Acorn's and Lightning's coats were glowing in the moonlight.

When they got to the barn, Lulu asked, "Which stall is Snow White in?"

"The last on the right," Pam answered.

Lulu was suddenly very anxious to be with Snow White. She dropped her sleeping bag and ran through the barn until she came to the last stall. Looking over the wooden gate, she saw Snow White standing in the corner. Her injured leg was wrapped in a huge bandage. Lulu also noticed little stitches dotting the pony's white coat like stiff black hairs. She felt sad for all that the pony had been through.

She went into the stall. "Hi, Snow White," she said quietly. "How are you feeling?"

Snow White didn't even look up.

Pam came in behind Lulu and said, "She must be very tired from everything."

"Look at all the stitches," Lulu whispered. "And her leg. How can she walk with that thing? It goes up over her hock. She can't bend her leg."

"That's the idea," Pam explained. "My dad says that the bandage is supposed to keep her leg stiff so the stitches will stay in place and the wound will heal." Then Pam went back outside to feed Acorn and Lightning.

While she was gone, Dr. Crandal came in to tell Lulu what to do for Snow White that night.

"We'll know that Snow White is on the road to recovery," Dr. Crandal concluded, "when she's eating and moving around."

When Dr. Crandal left, Lulu made a neat copy of his instructions.

To take care of Snow White tonight
1. Give plenty of water
2. Try to get S.W. to eat hay
3. Try to get S.W. to walk
4. Call doctor (on barn phone) if any questions or problems

Pam came back into the barn with Anna, who had arrived for the sleepover. While Snow White slept, the girls set up the empty stall next to Snow White's with their sleeping bags. Anna patted her backpack and said, "I brought over some quiches and kiwi tarts left over from the party my mother catered."

"Sometimes," Pam told Lulu, "Anna brings the weirdest things to school for lunch."

At the mention of school, they all said together, "What grade are you in?" Pam and Anna were asking Lulu. And Lulu was asking them.

They answered in unison, too. "Fifth grade."

All three girls laughed and hit high fives.

"How many fifth-grade classes are there?" Lulu asked.

"Only one," Anna said.

"So," Pam said, "we're all in the same class."

"And," Anna continued, "our teacher,

Mr. Livingston, is nice. You'll like him."

The girls yelled "All right!" and hit high fives again. They were all giggling. But not so loudly that they didn't hear Snow White neigh.

"She's awake!" Lulu shouted.

They ran to the pony's stall. Snow White was finally awake, but still standing in the corner. Lulu motioned the other two girls to stand back while she went up to the pony.

"It's all right, Snow White," Lulu said. "You're going to be okay. You probably feel a little drowsy from the medicine Dr. Crandal gave you. But you're going to be fine."

Snow White neighed again.

Lulu offered the pony water, but Snow White refused. Remembering their time together in the field, Lulu dipped into the pail and offered Snow White a slosh of water in her cupped hand. Snow White lapped the water. After that the pony drank more water from the pail.

"It would be a good sign," Lulu said, "if she'd eat and move around."

"Maybe it would work better if Lulu were alone with her," Anna suggested.

Pam agreed and the two girls started to leave the stall. Snow White snorted.

The three girls laughed.

Snow White whinnied and nodded her head, as if to say, "I want you all to stay."

"I think she likes the sound of our voices," Lulu said.

So for the next hour Pam, Anna, and Lulu visited with Snow White. The girls had so much to learn about one another that there wasn't a moment of silence.

Around ten o'clock Pam said they should go outside and check on Acorn and Lightning. "I'll stay here. I want to get Snow White to eat. And walk a little, too," Lulu said.

"I think we're babying her too much," Pam said. "If we leave her alone I bet she'll try to do more."

Anna took Lulu's hand and gave her a little pull. "Come on."

Lulu hated to leave Snow White, even for a little while. But if it meant that the pony might walk, she would go.

After the girls checked on Lightning and Acorn, they returned to the barn. Lulu was the first to see Snow White's head sticking out over the stall door.

"Snow White!" Lulu shouted as she ran toward the pony. "You walked!"

Snow White snorted at her, as if to say, "Where were you?"

Lulu stroked the pony's muzzle and said, "Good for you, Snow White."

A few minutes later Snow White was munching on hay.

Then Lulu got her to walk a few more steps. "I wonder if the stiff leg hurts when she walks?" Lulu asked.

"Probably," a man's voice answered. The girls and Snow White all turned to see Dr. Crandal standing at the stall door. He was smiling at them. "But with you three to distract her, she can't be feeling too badly."

Dr. Crandal was very impressed with the pony's progress. "This is a terrific pony," he said. "Somewhere along the line she's had good care and a lot of human company. She loves people."

"I guess it was that girl Rema," Lulu said.

"But her father doesn't care about Snow White one bit and he was so mean to Lulu, Dad."

"I just talked to Mr. Baxter," Dr. Crandal said. "He's been under a lot of stress with his new business. Also his wife's been in California because her father's in the hospital."

"That's no excuse for not trying to save an animal who's been hurt," Lulu said.

"Well," Dr. Crandal said, "with you girls taking care of her, this pony has a good chance for recovery."

Dr. Crandal told the girls they should let Snow White rest and get some sleep themselves.

Anna and Pam said good night to the pony. Lulu waited until Snow White was fast asleep before joining them in the stall they'd set up for their sleepover.

She found Anna and Pam still wide-awake and talking.

"Wouldn't it be wonderful," Anna said to Lulu, "if Snow White were your pony? Then we'd all have ponies."

Lulu got into her sleeping bag. "For now," she said, "let's pretend Snow White *is* my pony."

They all agreed and lay awake talking about all the things they'd do together on their ponies. It was a long list.

The Best Medicine

Anna and Pam were right about the fifth-grade class at Wiggins Elementary. The teacher — Mr. Livingston — was nice, and the other kids in the fifth grade were okay, too. But Lulu Sanders had only one thing on her mind during her first week at Wiggins Elementary. Snow White.

Every morning that week she got up at six o'clock. By six-thirty she was out of the house and riding an old bike she'd borrowed from Anna's older sister. She'd pedal through the chilly early morning mist to the Crandals' barn.

Lulu would run into the barn calling, "Morning, Snow White." The pony would show how happy she was to see Lulu by putting her head over the stall door and whinnying. After giving Snow White a fresh pail of water to drink, Lulu would muck out the pony's stall. Using a pitchfork, she removed the manure and the wet straw and put them in a wheelbarrow. Then she stacked the straw that wasn't soiled in a corner so she could sweep the floor.

Lulu would then add pitchforks of fresh, dry straw to the stall. She wanted Snow White to have an extra comfortable stall while her leg was healing.

Next, Lulu crushed up Snow White's pills and put them in her oats. She had to see that the pony ate all the oats so she'd get all the medicine.

While Lulu was taking care of Snow

White, Pam was also in the barn doing her morning chores.

Lulu's last two chores were to make sure there was hay and fresh water for Snow White to have during the day.

When Pam and Lulu finished in the barn, they washed up in the tack room and rode bikes together to school.

During the day, Dr. Crandal checked on Snow White. He'd take off the big bandage, see how the wound was healing, change the dressing, and put the bandage back on.

After school each day Lulu did everything for Snow White that she'd done in the morning — all over again. But in the afternoon she also had time to groom Snow White and hand-walk her in the barn. Every day Snow White walked a little farther down the aisle between the stalls.

Lulu made a chart to keep track of the chores she had to do for Snow White.

Friday afternoon, as Lulu and Pam

		Tues.	Wed.	Thurs.	Fri.
Muck out stall	A.M.	✓	✓	✓	✓
	P.M.	✓	✓	✓	
Lay in two sections of fresh hay	A.M.	✓	✓	✓	✓
	P.M.	✓	✓	✓	
Clean and refill water buckets	A.M.	✓	✓	✓	✓
	P.M.	✓	✓	✓	
Two handfuls of oats with pills	A.M.	✓	✓	✓	✓
	P.M.	✓	✓	✓	
Grooming	P.M.	✓	✓	✓	
Hand walk		2 min.	4 min.	6 min.	
Check leg and change dressing shot		✓	✓	✓	

turned their bikes onto Riddle Road, Lulu screamed. "Snow White's outside! Look, Pam."

They pumped hard on their bikes to get to the paddock as fast as they could. Pam's mother was leading Snow White slowly toward them. The twins sat on the paddock fence cheering Snow White on.

"Snow White!" Lulu shouted as she climbed over the fence and ran up to the pony.

Snow White nuzzled Lulu.

"Dr. Crandal is so impressed with her progress that we thought she should get some fresh air and a little walk today," Mrs. Crandal said as she smiled at Lulu. "I also thought it would be a nice surprise for you." She handed Lulu the lead rope and gave her a hug around the shoulders. "You've given Snow White the best medicine in the world, Lulu. T.L.C. Do you know what T.L.C. stands for?"

"Tender Loving Care," Lulu said.

Mrs. Crandal nodded. "That's right. Dr. Crandal says he's never seen a leg wound heal up so fast. You've done a super job of nursing, Lulu. Snow White's about ready to go home."

Lulu suddenly felt all the happiness drain out of her. "Go home?" she whispered. "You mean back to Mr. Baxter?"

"Snow White is his pony," Mrs. Crandal

74

said. "I'm sure he'll let you visit her. After all, you saved her life."

"He probably wishes Snow White died," Pam said, "so Lulu would have to pay and he wouldn't have to spend all his money."

"Now Pam," Mrs. Crandal said, "be fair. According to your father, Mr. Baxter's been under a lot of pressure lately."

Lulu could hear Pam and her mother talking, but she wasn't paying any attention to what they said. She was looking into Snow White's eyes. "I'll still take care of you, Snow White," she whispered. "I promise. I'll find a way."

"Acorn! Acorn!" Jack and Jill were shouting. Lulu saw that Anna and her Shetland pony were coming off Pony Pal Trail. The twins raced one another to open the paddock gate. Lightning whinnied as she ran along the fence of the side paddock. She was greeting Acorn, too.

Snow White snorted, but not happily. "It's okay, Snow White," Lulu said. "Lightning and Acorn are your pals."

Mrs. Crandal said Anna should put Acorn in the side paddock with Lightning. "Until they get used to Snow White and she gets used to them," she said. "Especially since Snow White has an injury."

Mrs. Crandal went back to the animal clinic to finish her day's work. The twins joined Lightning and Acorn in the side paddock. And the three friends sat in a row on the paddock fence near Snow White.

"This is the first time our ponies are together," Anna said. "Even though they're in different paddocks you can see them all at once. Three ponies. Three girls. Six Pony Pals."

"Five Pony Pals," Lulu said. "I can't pretend that Snow White is mine anymore. She's going back to the Baxters."

Pam jumped off the fence and shouted, "It isn't fair." She put her hands on her hips and faced Anna and Lulu. "Mr. Baxter doesn't want a pony and doesn't have time to take care of her. Lulu wants a pony and

does have the time to take care of her. The fair thing is that Lulu should have the pony."

"Especially because she saved Snow White's life," Anna said.

"You're both acting like Snow White is Mr. Baxter's pony," Lulu said. "But really she is Rema's pony."

A car pulled into the driveway. Lulu figured it was someone going to the animal clinic, but Pam recognized the car. "He's here," she said.

"Who?" Lulu and Anna asked.

"Mr. Baxter," Pam answered. "And there's someone with him."

Lulu jumped down from the fence and stood next to Snow White like she was the pony's bodyguard. She watched Mr. Baxter and a woman get out of the car.

As soon as the woman saw Snow White she ran ahead of Mr. Baxter calling, "Snow White. Oh poor Snow White."

Snow White turned toward the voice and

whinnied. Lulu knew by the happy sound in the whinny and the curl of the pony's lips that Snow White liked the woman.

"Are you the girl who saved Snow White's life?" the woman asked.

"Yes," Lulu said.

The woman had tears in her eyes. "I'm Mrs. Baxter," she said. "We're all so grateful. Rema's been worried sick about Snow White. We've all been so worried."

Lulu noticed that Mr. Baxter didn't even say hello to Snow White. He just looked at the big bandage and shook his head in disgust.

Mrs. Crandal joined the group at the paddock fence. After she introduced herself, she explained to the Baxters that Snow White could go home. She told them, "In another week the bandage will be removed. But you must understand that it will be months before she's as strong and limber as she was before the accident."

Lulu noticed that Mr. Baxter's face got

that angry look again. "So, she still needs a lot of care," he said.

Mrs. Crandal agreed. "The vet should check her every day until the bandage is off. After that she'll need leg soaks. And, of course, regular exercise."

Mrs. Baxter turned to her husband. "We're at work all day. And the fence needs to be replaced."

"Maybe you should leave Snow White here," Pam said.

Mr. Baxter shook his head. "Boarding an animal is expensive."

"Lulu's been taking care of Snow White for free," Mrs. Crandal explained. "And doing a wonderful job. We're only charging you for medical care and food."

"I love ponies and I know a lot about them from when I lived in England," Lulu said. She stroked Snow White's neck. Snow White lovingly nuzzled Lulu's shoulder.

"Lulu knows as much about ponies as I do and I grew up with them," Pam said.

The Baxters looked at one another and nodded in agreement. "We'll leave Snow White here for another three weeks," Mrs. Baxter said.

The Pony Pals cheered — and hugged Snow White.

Whose Pony Is It?

After the Baxters left, Lulu led Snow White back to her stall. As she rubbed her down she told her, "Snow White, you're my pony for another three weeks."

"We've got to do better than that," Pam said. Lulu looked up to see her two friends leaning on the stall gate.

"We should think real hard about how Snow White can be Lulu's pony," Anna said.

"We would have so much fun if you had a pony too, Lulu," Pam said.

Lulu pictured them all riding on Pony Pal Trail. Anna was on her feisty Shetland, the little brown Acorn. Pam was on her sleek Connemara, the red Lightning. And she was on the sweetest Welsh pony in the world, Snow White. Lulu couldn't think of anything that would make her happier.

"My mother invited both you guys to dinner," Pam said.

"I can't," Lulu said. "My grandmother's doing my hair tonight. I can't put it off any longer."

Anna imitated Lulu's grandmother. "Oh, Lucinda dear, we must do something with that hair. I think a lovely purple color and a few million curls would be nice."

They all giggled. "Okay, you guys," Lulu said. "Just promise you won't laugh when you see me tomorrow."

Pam turned very serious. "Tomorrow," she said, "we should each have a plan for how we can get Snow White for Lulu. For keeps. Write out your idea."

*　　*　　*

Two hours later Grandmother was combing out Lulu's freshly washed hair. Lulu could see Grandmother's stern expression in the mirror when she asked Lulu, "How much longer will you be taking care of the Baxter girl's horse?"

"Just another couple of weeks," Lulu said.

"I don't like it," Grandmother scolded. "The Baxters should be taking care of their own animal." Grandmother picked up the scissors and began cutting.

"When you cut Rema Baxter's hair, what was she like?" Lulu asked.

"Let me see," Grandmother answered. "Her hair's a beautiful dark brown. Nice and thick."

Lulu interrupted. "I meant what's *she* like. Was she nice? Or did she act like a snob?"

"Rema Baxter was very mannerly," Grandmother said. "She seemed excited about going away to boarding school. She said Wiggins was too small for her. She's attending an excellent school."

Lulu turned toward her grandmother and asked excitedly, "Do you know the name and everything?" she said.

"My dear!" Grandmother said with alarm. "Do stay still. I almost cut your ear-lobe just then."

"Sorry," Lulu said. She turned back to the mirror and talked to her grandmother's reflection. "What's the name of Rema's school, Grandma?"

"She attends Clinton Hall," Grandmother said. "A private girls' academy in Delaware."

Clinton Hall in Delaware. Lulu repeated it to herself so she wouldn't forget.

The next morning the Pony Pals met at the Crandals'. Since Acorn and Lightning were grazing in the main paddock, Lulu put Snow White in the side one. Anna and Pam were sitting on the grass with their backs against the fence waiting for her. As Lulu came toward her friends, Anna called, "Your hair looks great."

"No purple," Lulu said.

"And no fake curls," Pam added.

The Pony Pals laughed.

"Okay, everyone, take out your plans for getting Snow White for Lulu," Pam said.

Lulu noticed that Snow White was cautiously making her way toward the fence that divided her from Lightning and Acorn.

Lulu said, "Let's hear yours first, Pam."

Pam unfolded a piece of paper and read.

Lulu buys Snow White with her allowance money.

"It's a perfect idea," Pam said. "Didn't Mr. Baxter say he wished he'd sold Snow White already?"

"He didn't sell her because of Rema, remember?" Lulu said. "And Mrs. Baxter seems to really like Snow White, too."

"If Lulu spends all her money buying Snow White, how can she pay to keep her?" Anna asked. "Don't forget that it costs money to feed a pony, especially in the winter."

"Plus," Lulu said, "my father's project in the Amazon ends in June. I'll be leaving Wiggins."

"I didn't know that," Pam said.

"Me either," Anna said.

Both girls looked very sad.

Lulu liked her new friends so much that she felt sad herself. She asked, "So, what's your idea, Anna?"

Anna unfolded a piece of drawing paper. "I drew mine," she said.

"My idea," Anna explained, "is that Lulu should rent Snow White from the Baxters. That's not as expensive as buying her.

We're leasing Acorn. Lots of people lease ponies. And Snow White can live with Acorn in his paddock. My parents said it'd be okay. There's plenty of room in the pony shelter, too."

"What a great idea," Pam said. "That way Acorn will have a stablemate. My dad said that Acorn's always trying to get out of his paddock because he's lonely."

"So it would be good for Acorn and it would be good for Snow White," Anna said.

"And it'd be perfect for Rema," Lulu added. "She comes home for the summer just about the same time as I'm leaving." Lulu didn't let herself think too much about how sad it would be to part with Snow White in June. She needed to use all her energy to figure out how she could have her until then.

"But there's a problem," Lulu told Anna and Pam. "I'd have to buy a saddle and helmet. Bridles, too. All that tack stuff is expensive."

"Maybe you could rent Rema's tack from the Baxters," Pam said.

"Great idea," Lulu said.

"Look!" Anna was pointing toward the ponies.

The girls looked up to see that Acorn and Snow White were nose to nose at the fence separating the two paddocks. "They're getting to know one another by smelling each other's breath," Pam explained. "They'd make great stablemates."

"What was your idea?" Anna asked Lulu.

Lulu handed Anna a piece of paper. "It fits right in with your idea," she said. "Read it out loud."

Anna wouldn't take the paper. "No," she said. "It's your idea. You read it."

Lulu read:

Write a letter to Rema Baxter and ask her if I can take care of Snow White while she's at school. Also tell her that I'd like to ride Snow White.

"Perfect," Pam said. "I bet the Baxters will agree to let you take care of Snow White if Rema says it's okay. Let's write the letter right now."

"Great," Lulu said. "Then we can get the school's address from the library."

When they'd finished the letter, Pam said, "It's a good letter. We got everything in."

"I like that you signed it 'Lucinda,'" Anna said. "And used big words like, 'proper arrangements.' If she's as stuck-up as I think she is, she'll love that stuff."

"What about when she comes home for vacations?" Pam asked. "Won't she want to ride her pony?"

Lulu added a P.S. to the letter saying that during vacations, Snow White could stay at Rema's. She also reminded Rema that the paddock fence should be replaced.

"Just one more thing," Lulu told her friends. She added a P.P.S. and read it aloud. "Snow White says 'Hi.'"

"Now," Pam said, "it's a perfect letter."

On Pony Pal Trail

The first thing Lulu did after school every day was to flip through the pile of mail on the kitchen counter. Day after day she was disappointed. There was no mail for her. No letter from Rema.

And every day while having an afternoon snack in the beauty parlor, she'd ask her grandmother, "Did I get any calls today?"

Grandmother would say, "No, dear. Are you expecting a call?"

And Lulu would say, "Just wondered."

As the days went by, Snow White was getting stronger and stronger. And so was Lulu's love for her.

Meanwhile Lulu wasn't spending any of her allowance money. She'd figured out that leasing a pony and paying for feed would cost more than twenty-five dollars a week. This worried her. What if Rema and her parents said she could lease Snow White and she couldn't afford it?

Three weeks passed this way.

It was a Saturday afternoon. Lulu was in Acorn's stall helping Anna give him an extra-special grooming before going over to Pam's on Pony Pal Trail.

"I can't believe Rema hasn't answered my letter," Lulu said.

Anna looked up from combing out Acorn's mane. "I told you she was a snob."

"But my grandmother said Rema had good manners," Lulu said.

"With grown-ups maybe," Anna said. "But I bet she's not nice to other kids."

"You're probably right," Lulu said. "I bet she thinks I'm just this little kid who's too young to take care of her pony."

"Lucinda! Lucinda!" Grandmother was yelling to Lulu from the back steps. "Come in, dear. To the beauty parlor."

Lulu shouted "Coming!" to her grandmother. She put down the rub cloth she was using on Acorn and said, "She probably wants me to go to the store. I'll come back as fast as I can."

When Lulu came into the beauty parlor, Grandmother looked up from the head of brown hair that she was cutting. She pointed her scissors at the corner of the desk and said, "A letter came for you. From Rema Baxter. You've been so interested in the mail lately, I thought you'd want to know right away."

Lulu already had the letter in her hand. "Thanks, Grandma," she said as she ran from the beauty parlor.

Grandmother called after her, "Lucinda, no running . . ."

But Lulu was already out the door and on her way back to Anna's.

She was breathless when she got there. "I got a letter from Rema," she said. She handed Anna the letter. "You open it and read it to me. I'm too nervous."

Anna opened the letter much too slowly for Lulu's taste. Finally she pulled out the letter. And handed it to Lulu.

"It's a letter written to you," she said. "You read it."

Lulu read:

Dear Lucinda:

My parents and I have discussed your offer to lease Snow White. We propose the following business arrangement.

1. Lucinda Sanders takes care of Snow White in a paddock to be inspected by Mrs. Baxter.

2. Lucinda Sanders pays for Snow White's feed. All other expenses to be paid for by Mr. and Mrs. Baxter.

3. Lucinda Sanders will send a monthly written report on Snow White's health to me.
4. There will be no leasing fee.

If you agree to the above tell my parents.

By the way my parents are the only ones who call me "Rema." Everyone else calls me "Rae." Do you have a nickname?

Sincerely,

Rae

P.S.
I forgot to say that you can borrow my tack. But it must be maintained in good condition.
P.P.S.
Give Snow White a big hug and kiss from me.

When Lulu finished reading the letter, she and Anna hugged one another and jumped up and down. Then, suddenly, Lulu stopped and became serious.

"What's wrong?" Anna said. "It couldn't be more perfect."

"My grandmother has to agree," Lulu said. "And you know how she feels about ponies."

"Show her Rema's letter," Anna suggested. "It's a very proper letter and your grandmother likes that sort of thing."

Again Lulu ran through the paddock, over the fence, through Grandmother's yard, and into the house. She walked through the dining room and into the beauty parlor. Lulu handed her Grandmother the letter.

When she'd finished reading, Grandmother tapped the letter with a comb and said, "Lucinda, what would your father say to all this? I mean if you were able to reach him and ask his permission to have a pony."

Lulu told her grandmother, "Dad would say it was wonderful. That it was a great opportunity to have a pony without spending a lot of money. Dad would say that taking care of an animal will teach me responsibility. He'd say that I'm a good rider and I know a lot about ponies."

"Yes," Grandmother agreed, "he would say all those things." She handed the letter back to Lulu. "Well, I suppose it will be easier if the animal is right next door. I don't like you riding about on that bicycle so early in the morning."

Lulu hugged her grandmother. "Thank you. Thank you," she gushed.

A few minutes later Lulu was walking and jogging beside Anna and Acorn as they rode on Pony Pal Trail toward the Crandals'.

"I can't believe that Snow White is mine," Lulu said. "Until June anyway."

"We're going to have so much fun," Anna said. "I'm so glad it's you and Snow White and not Rema and Snow White. Don't you think she sounded snobby in that letter?"

"I thought it was the most wonderful letter in the world," Lulu said. "And her name is 'Rae.' We should call her that from now on."

They both saw Pam and Lightning coming toward them from the opposite direction on Pony Pal Trail.

"Yes! Yes! Yes!" Pam shouted. "It's the best news I've ever heard."

"I called and told Pam right away," Anna said.

"That's okay," Lulu said. "As long as I'm the one who tells Snow White."

Lulu gave Lightning a pat on the neck as she asked Pam, "Did Anna tell you everything that Rae said?"

"Who's Rae?" Pam asked.

"Rae is this stuck-up name Reina wants everyone to call her," Anna said.

Pam and Lulu laughed.

"Anna, how can you hate someone you don't even know?" Lulu asked.

"I have a feeling about her. I think she's a — "

" — snob." Pam and Lulu completed the sentence with her.

It seemed to Lulu that Pam was taking forever to turn Lightning around. And Anna was having trouble getting Acorn to stop grazing and get moving. "I'll meet you guys there," Lulu said.

As she ran along the trail at her fastest pace, Lulu was remembering the first time she was on Pony Pal Trail and how she'd wished she had a pony to ride.

When the woods opened up to the paddock, Lulu saw that Snow White was waiting for her. "Snow White!" she called. "Snow White, I've got the best news."

As she ran to Snow White, she saw that the pony had a bit in her mouth and a saddle on her back. Mrs. Crandal was standing nearby holding the reins. "She's strong enough to be ridden now," she said.

"Are you sure?" Lulu asked.

Mrs. Crandal nodded. "For just a short walk. You can go out a little longer each day."

Lulu patted Snow White and said, "I'll

take the best care of you, Snow White. I really will. I love you."

Anna and Acorn and Pam and Lightning came off the trail and stopped near Lulu and Snow White.

Lulu looked up at them. Anna and Pam were grinning from ear to ear. Pam said, "As soon as Anna called with the good news, we went right to the Baxters' to get the tack. That's Rema's — I mean Rae's — saddle and bridle."

Lulu tightened the girth around Snow White's stomach.

"Lulu, do you want me to give you a leg up?" Mrs. Crandal asked.

"I can mount by myself," Lulu said. She put her left foot in the stirrup and in a swift, graceful movement hoisted herself up onto her pony.

She adjusted the stirrups, took proper hold of the reins, and balanced herself in the saddle.

"Snow White is the perfect size for you Lulu," Pam said.

Looking straight ahead between Snow White's alert ears, Lulu saw that they were facing the open gate to Pony Pal Trail.

She took a deep breath, squeezed her calves against Snow White's sides, and said, "Okay, Snow White, let's go for a ride."

A Pony for Keeps

For Anika Marissa Murray

The author thanks Elvia Gignoux for generously sharing her lifelong knowledge and love of horses.

Thanks also to Shirley Kokesh and the fifth-grade girls at Kildonan Elementary School, particularly Hannah Charlap.

1

The Woman in Red

Anna Harley sat tall in the saddle. She looked over her pony's head at her two friends and the trail ahead. Anna loved riding on Pony Pal Trail. This is going to be a great day, she thought. I'm going to have a good time and not think about my problem.

Whenever the Pony Pals went out with their ponies they took turns in the lead position. This sunny winter morning Pam Crandal was in the lead on her tall chestnut-colored pony, Lightning. Behind her was

Lulu Sanders on Snow White. Then came Anna on her little brown and black Shetland pony, Acorn.

The Pony Pals reached a long, straight stretch of trail. Pam moved Lightning into a trot and then a canter. Lulu and Snow White picked up their pace. Anna squeezed her legs against Acorn's side. "Come on, Acorn," she said. "Faster."

But Acorn slowed down instead.

Anna patiently waited for him to decide whether to keep up with the others.

Suddenly Acorn snorted and charged ahead so fast that Anna thought they might climb right up Snow White's back. "Whoa," Anna called out as she shifted her position in the saddle and pulled on the reins. But, as usual, Acorn stopped when *he* decided that it was time to stop.

Lulu turned Snow White around to face Anna and Acorn. "Is Acorn being the boss again today?" Lulu asked.

Anna felt a little embarrassed that she

couldn't always control her pony. But she joked, "So what else is new?"

Pam turned Lightning around to face the other Pony Pals. "Let's go onto the Wiggins estate," she said excitedly. She pointed to a space between the trees. "We can get on a trail over there." Lightning pawed the ground and whinnied as if to agree.

"But look," Lulu said, "there's some new *No Trespassing* signs."

"They're for hunters," Pam said. "Not for kids on their ponies."

"The riding trails are great in there," Lulu added. "We had fun the last time we went."

Anna looked from Pam to Lulu. "You guys just want to jump your ponies," she said.

"These are the best conditions we've had this winter for jumping," Pam said. "No snow. No ice. No mud."

Lulu leaned over and stroked Snow White's smooth white neck. "Snow White loves to jump."

"Come on, Anna," Pam said. "Maybe today's the day Acorn will finally jump for you."

Lulu reached over and scratched Acorn's neck through his black mane. "We all know you can do it, Acorn," she said.

"Okay," Anna finally agreed. "Let's go."

Even though Acorn wouldn't jump, Anna had fun on the trails. Her little pony was surefooted and smart. He loved the challenge of finding ways around the fallen logs that Lightning and Snow White jumped over. I could go almost anywhere on my pony, Anna thought. He's clever and brave. Who cares if he won't jump for me?

The Pony Pals went farther into the Wiggins estate than they'd ever gone before. After awhile they got off their ponies and let them drink from Badd Brook. Through the leafless trees the girls could see Wiggins mansion in the distance.

"That Wiggins lady must be so weird to live in a big place like that all by herself," Anna said. "I heard it has twenty-seven rooms, not counting the bathrooms."

"I bet she hasn't left there in twenty-seven years," Lulu said.

"And has at least twenty-seven cats," Pam added.

"And hasn't taken a bath in twenty-seven weeks," Anna kidded. "Or brushed her teeth."

"Gross!" they all screamed. The Pony Pals giggled.

Suddenly Anna stopped laughing. "I wonder what she would do if she found us here?"

"Probably take us prisoners," Pam teased. "Like Hansel and Gretel."

Lulu cackled like a witch. "I'll eat you up, my pretties."

"You guys," Anna whispered. "Someone's riding a horse out of the barn. *Look*."

Anna pointed to a distant shape. She could make out that it was a rider dressed in red on a big black horse.

"I bet it's her," Lulu said.

"And she's coming this way," Pam added. "Let's get out of here."

The girls quickly mounted their ponies and galloped toward Pony Pal Trail.

Even though he was the smallest, Acorn kept up with Snow White and Lightning. As they galloped along Anna thought, Acorn, you always come through for me when it's really important.

When the girls reached Pony Pal Trail, Anna and Lulu said good-bye to Pam. The woodland trail connected Acorn's and Snow White's paddock with Lightning's paddock.

Pam and Lightning headed toward her house at the north end of Pony Pal Trail. Anna and Lulu waved and then walked their ponies along. "Tonight I'll write to Rema Baxter and tell her that we practiced jumping," Lulu said.

Anna remembered how the Pony Pals helped Snow White recover from her terrible accident. And then how they worked together to convince Rema Baxter and her parents to let Lulu take care of Snow White.

"You shouldn't have to keep writing all

that stuff down," Anna said. "It's like Rema's giving you homework. She should just be thankful you saved Snow White's life."

"She is," Lulu said. "That's why she's letting me take care of Snow White until she gets back from boarding school."

"How could Rema leave Snow White just for a chance to go to a different school?" Anna asked.

"Maybe it's a really good school and she likes to study or something," Lulu said.

Anna couldn't imagine giving up Acorn for schoolwork. Then she remembered the problem she'd managed to forget about all morning. Tears sprung to her eyes as the awful truth came back to her. *She* was going to have to give up *her* pony because of school, too. Only in her case the problem was because she hated school, not because she loved it.

The Wrong Pony

Back at their ponies' shelter, Anna and Lulu removed saddles and bridles. Then they led the ponies out into the paddock they shared behind Anna's house. Anna watched Snow White run after Acorn to a far corner of the field.

Anna loved that the ponies got along so well. Just like the Pony Pals, she thought.

Anna and Pam had been best friends since kindergarten. Pam liked to be in charge and was very smart. She always did well in school. Pam was really smart about animals, too, especially horses. She'd been around them all her life because her dad was a large-animal veterinarian and her mother was a riding instructor.

Anna thought about her other best friend, Lulu. Lulu and her dad lived in England for two years. That's where Lulu learned all about ponies and how to ride them. Now Lulu was staying with her grandmother in the house next door. Lulu's father was studying wildlife in the Amazon jungle while Lulu was living in Wiggins. Anna knew that Lulu missed her father a lot. She was really close to her dad, especially because her mother died when she was four. Lulu wasn't sad though; she was a happy, adventurous person. She loved exploring nature like her father and had great ideas about things to do outdoors.

Anna thought about her own parents. Her father built houses, so he got to work outdoors. Her mother worked indoors because she owned a diner and catered parties. Anna was the person in her family who loved animals the most. She especially liked ponies.

In the paddock Snow White and Acorn were nose to nose, sniffing, nibbling, and nickering at one another. Anna thought, The Pony Pals are three best friends with three wonderful ponies. Now I'm going to spoil it.

"Look at Acorn and Snow White," Lulu said. "It's sad to think that they'll be separated when Rema comes home."

"They're going to be separated sooner than that," Anna mumbled.

"Why?" Lulu asked. "Did your parents say Snow White can't stay here?"

"Snow White can stay," Anna said. "It's Acorn who has to leave."

Lulu was shocked. "Why does Acorn have to leave?" she asked.

"Because I don't do good in school like you and Pam," Anna explained. "My parents said they won't let me buy Acorn unless my marks go up. When report cards come out I'll have to give him back to the man we leased him from."

"You can get better marks, Anna," Lulu said. "You're really smart. You get low marks because you don't like to write. Listen — Pam and I will help you get ready for the unit tests next week."

Anna didn't tell Lulu that no matter how much she studied, she still couldn't get passing grades on tests. She had no trouble understanding what went on in class but she couldn't do the written work. And she could hardly read a sentence without coming across words she didn't know.

Their fifth-grade teacher, Mr. Livingston, gave her extra homework in reading and math. But it wasn't working. She still made the same dumb mistakes. Sometimes she got so fed up that she just doodled and made pictures of ponies.

"Why didn't you tell me about this before?" Lulu asked. "Pam and I could have been helping you all this time."

"I don't know," Anna said. "I just didn't."

That night as Anna said good night to

118

Acorn, she thought about why she didn't tell Lulu and Pam. She knew it was because she felt ashamed that she couldn't read or write like her friends. "Oh, Acorn," Anna said, "maybe, just maybe, the Pony Pals *can* help me." Anna stroked Acorn's neck. "If I study out loud with them maybe I'll get better marks on that stupid report card." She gave Acorn a big hug good night. "Then I can keep you."

Sunday morning, after chores, Anna and Lulu saddled up their ponies and rode over to Pam's place on Pony Pal Trail. Pam's five-year-old twin brother and sister, Jack and Jill, were waiting for them.

"Can I ride Acorn?" they shouted together.

Anna laughed and told Mrs. Crandal she didn't mind if the twins rode her pony. "Thanks so much," Mrs. Crandal said. "I'd love to give them a chance to ride."

"It'll be fun for Acorn, too," said Anna.

Mrs. Crandal went to the barn to get two

riding helmets. A few minutes later, the Pony Pals watched her and the twins go onto the trail with Acorn.

"Would you ride Snow White?" Lulu asked Anna. "Rema said other people should ride her so she doesn't become too attached to me."

"Rema Baxter's nutty," Anna said. "But I'll do it for you."

Even though Snow White was quite a bit higher than Acorn, Anna swung easily into the saddle. She adjusted the stirrups to her own height and then rode around the outside of the field. Anna was amazed at how responsive Snow White was to her commands. It took only the slightest shift in her weight and a squeeze of her legs to move from a walk to a trot to a canter.

Then, almost without thinking, Anna turned Snow White to the center of the field. They faced three low jumps that Mrs. Crandal had set up. Anna directed Snow White over them. Jumping felt wonderful. Anna felt as if she and Snow White were

floating. Anna remembered how much she loved jumping in riding school.

As she slowed Snow White down to a walk, Anna looked anxiously toward Pony Pal Trail. She was relieved that Acorn hadn't seen her riding and jumping on another pony. She didn't want his feelings to be hurt.

Lulu and Pam clapped for Anna and Snow White.

"I forgot what a terrific jumper you are, Anna," Pam said. "You have great timing and balance."

"Wow," Lulu said. "I didn't even know you could jump. Why won't Acorn do jumps?"

"I don't know," Anna said.

"Maybe Acorn's just the wrong pony for you, Anna," Pam suggested.

Anna answered angrily, "Acorn is the *right* pony for me." She dismounted Snow White and handed the reins to Lulu. "Jumping is no big deal."

Eight Homes in Twelve Years

"I've schooled a lot of ponies," Mrs. Crandal said. "But I've never met one quite as stubborn as your Acorn." The Pony Pals were sitting in the Crandals' kitchen eating lunch.

Anna felt angry at everyone — including Mrs. Crandal — for criticizing Acorn. She felt a little better when Mrs. Crandal added, "And I've never met a pony quite as smart. I wonder who owned him before and how he was treated. Did you lease him from Reggie Olson?"

Anna nodded.

"Who's Reggie Olson?" Lulu asked.

"Reggie Olson has a big horse farm over on Crosshill Road," Pam explained. "A lot of people with horses around here get them from him."

"What's his farm like?" Lulu asked.

"Oh it's the neatest place," Anna answered. She was remembering the happy day when she looked at five pretty ponies in a field and picked out Acorn — the cutest one of all.

"You know," Mrs. Crandal said. "I haven't been over to Olson's place in ages. And we'll be getting the twins their first ponies soon. It'd be fun to check out his stock."

"And we could find out more about Acorn," Pam said.

Mrs. Crandal and the three girls made a plan. The next day she and the twins would pick them up after school and go together over to the Olson farm. But that was tomorrow. Right now the Pony Pals had some studying to do. They went up to Pam's room and took out their schoolbooks.

"Just stick with us," Lulu told Anna, "and you'll ace the tests."

Anna tried very hard to believe Lulu. And she tried very hard to study with her friends.

First they quizzed one another on science vocabulary. Anna learned the meanings easily when they drilled them out loud. But she was too embarrassed to tell her friends that she couldn't read some of words.

"Let's review math," Lulu suggested.

When Pam read a word problem out loud, Anna knew how to get the answer. But she couldn't remember the multiplication tables she needed to finish the problem.

Later, as Anna and Lulu mounted their ponies to ride home, Pam said, "Anna, you should write the times tables out five times each tonight."

"Maybe you should say them out loud as you write," Lulu added.

Anna didn't tell them that the week before she'd written out all the times tables *ten* times each.

The next afternoon, the Pony Pals were rushing to get their jackets from their lockers. They were excited to go to Olson's farm.

"How'd you do on the math test?" Lulu asked Anna.

"Okay," Anna said, even though she worked so slowly she'd only finished half the test.

Pam patted her on the back. "That's great. I just know you'll be able to keep Acorn."

The Olson farm was even bigger than Anna remembered. There were three paddocks with horses and ponies. And a yellow barn with clean, brightly lit horse stalls.

"I guess the last time I was here I only paid attention to Acorn," Anna said. "I don't remember seeing all those horses."

Mr. Olson, a white-haired man in jeans

and a plaid jacket, gave them a t
paddocks and barns.

The twins were picking out th
they wanted. Sometimes the same
saw that red one first so it's mine," Jill
shouted excitedly.

"It's already mine," Jack said. "I saw it
first. I just didn't tell you."

Mrs. Crandal reminded her children that
they weren't getting ponies that day. "Or
ever," she scolded, "if you two don't stop
arguing."

Mr. Olson walked over to the Pony Pals.
He smiled at Anna. "How's Acorn doing?"
he asked.

"Okay," Anna answered.

"We were wondering why Acorn's so
bossy," Lulu said.

"He's not bossy," Anna said. "He just has
a mind of his own."

"Maybe you want to be riding a horse
instead of a pony," Mr. Olson said. He
pointed to a handsome black horse looking

over the paddock fence. "That Morgan is a honey. Shouldn't be too big for you. I'd be happy to get Acorn back. I have another family looking to buy a pony just like him."

"I'm not too big for Acorn," Anna said. "And I won't be for a long time. Maybe never. Everyone in my family is short."

"Does that mean you'll be wanting to buy him then?" Mr. Olson asked.

"Yes," Anna answered. Her heart was pounding in her chest. I have to keep Acorn, she thought, I just have to.

"Well then," Mr. Olson said, "I might as well go over to the office and print out the terms of the sale. You can take the papers home with you. Save me the stamp." He turned and walked away.

Pam signaled to Lulu and Anna that they should go with Mr. Olson. Mr. Olson seemed surprised that the girls were walking alongside him toward the office.

Anna had an idea why Acorn was so strong-willed. "Has Acorn had a lot of

different people leasing him?" she asked Mr. Olson.

"As ponies go," he said thoughtfully, "I'd have to say Acorn's had quite a few homes."

"Didn't anyone ever want to buy him before?" Lulu asked.

"One family bought him a couple of years ago. But they moved to a big city and couldn't keep him. So I bought him back." With that, Mr. Olson opened the door to his office. The girls came in behind him.

He went over to his computer. "This will only take a minute," he said. The three girls watched him type T-E-R-M-S O-F S-A-L-E on the computer keyboard.

"Do you have a list of all the people Acorn's lived with?" Anna asked.

"Sure I do," he answered.

"I just love computers," Pam said. She winked at Lulu and Anna. "Could you show us how you keep the names of all the people who've leased or owned Acorn?"

Mr. Olson liked showing off his computer program almost as much as he liked

130

showing off his ponies and horses. The three girls hovered over his shoulder and watched the screen as he typed A-C-O-R-N. In a split second, a list of eight names and addresses appeared on the screen.

Even Mr. Olson was surprised at how many names were listed. "Eight homes in twelve years," he said. "That's a lot of different places for one pony to live. But that Shetland is tough."

Anna wondered what it was like for Acorn to have lived in so many different homes and to have had so many owners. They must have all treated him differently. And just when he got used to one family, he'd be moved to another. She saw that her own name and address were at the end of the list. Whose name would come next?

Mr. Olson typed again and said, "Miss Harley, do you want to buy the saddle and bridle with the pony?"

"Yes," Anna answered.

A few minutes later Mr. Olson printed

out two copies of the terms of the sale. He put them in an envelope and handed it to Anna. "If your parents have any questions have them give me a call," he told her. "As soon as they give me back a signed copy with a check, Acorn is yours."

Anna took the papers. I've got to get good grades on my report card, she thought. I have to keep Acorn.

When the Pony Pals were outside they tried to remember the list of people who had leased or owned Acorn. All Anna could remember was how sad the long list made her feel.

"I noticed that only two of the people he lived with were from Wiggins," Pam said.

"Didn't you guys see?" Lulu asked excitedly. "Tommy Rand was on that list!"

"Tommy Rand?" Anna asked. "Are you sure?"

"I'm sure," Lulu said. "He leased Acorn four years ago."

"Poor Acorn!" Anna exclaimed.

*　　*　　*

The girls talked about Tommy Rand all the way home from Olson's farm.

"He's the meanest eighth-grader," Pam said.

"The bossiest, too," Lulu added. "I hate how he orders us around when he's recess monitor."

"Acorn hates bossy people," Anna said.

"Maybe he was nicer when he was younger," Lulu suggested.

"Or nicer to animals than people," Pam added. "I meet lots of people at our animal clinic who are like that."

"I doubt it," Anna said. "But I have to find out for sure."

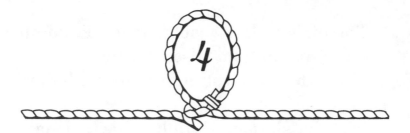

What Tommy Rand Said

The next day, as the three Pony Pals slowly moved along the school cafeteria line, Lulu whispered into Anna's ear, "There he is."

Anna looked up to see the tall, mean-looking Tommy Rand walking across the cafeteria with a lunch tray. She was scared, but she was determined to find out how Tommy Rand treated Acorn.

Anna reached Tommy Rand as he sat down at a table with the other eighth-grade boys.

"Hi," she said. She held up her notebook. "I'm Anna Harley and I'm doing a report on kids and their animals. I would like to interview you."

"Why me?" Tommy Rand said. "Ask someone your own age."

Anna persisted. "I know you had a Shetland pony when you were in the fourth grade. I was wondering if you could tell me what the pony was like."

"That was just a kid thing," he said. "I don't even remember its name."

Anna was so shocked at this that she blurted out, "Don't you *miss* him?"

She realized that Lulu and Pam were now standing next to her. Her friends made her feel more confident. "His name is Acorn," she told Tommy Rand.

"Did he ever jump for you?" Lulu asked.

"Why did you send him back to Mr. Olson?" Pam asked. "Why didn't you keep Acorn? Were you too lazy to take care of him?"

"Get lost," Tommy Rand said.

The eighth-grade boys were laughing so hard that the lunchroom teacher had to come over to quiet them down. But by then the Pony Pals were boldly marching to the fifth-grade table on the other side of the room.

Anna didn't care that everyone was staring at them. All she cared about was that she had to pass her science test that afternoon. No matter what, she had to protect Acorn from ever, ever having to be around another kid like Tommy Rand.

Even while they ate, Pam and Lulu helped Anna review the science lesson on the parts of the flower.

After dinner that night Anna told her mother, "I'm going out to check on the ponies."

"You better get to your homework," her father said.

Anna held up a folder and a flashlight. "I'll study out there," she said.

"Don't you think you'll be able to concentrate better in your room, at your desk?" her father asked.

"Just remember," her mother warned. "If your grades haven't gone up, no more pony."

Anna's older sister Tammy looked up from her magazine. "Can't you guys just leave her alone? Maybe she's doing the best she can."

"I doubt it," their father said. He put his arm around Anna and gave her a hug. "I know this girl. Her brain's as good as yours and her brother's. All my kids are smart. Anna's too easily distracted and draws when she should be writing. Seems to me that Acorn is the biggest distraction of all."

Anna wiggled away from her father's hug and went toward the back door. "Be right back," she said. She bolted out of the house full of anger and sadness.

Anna felt better after she ran through the yard and climbed the fence into the paddock. It was a beautiful night. The stars were sparkling in the dark sky.

It wasn't too cold for Anna in the shelter. Not with two warm ponies nearby. She sat on an empty feed bucket. Acorn came right over and nuzzled against her shoulder.

"How you doing, sweet pony?" she asked.

Acorn whinnied happily.

"You're right," she said. "I do have a treat for you." She reached in her pocket and gave Acorn an apple. Snow White, who'd been sleeping standing up on the other side of the shelter, woke up and came trotting over to her.

Anna laughed. "You were sleeping," she told the white pony. "How did you know I had an apple for you?" Snow White ate her apple. When she was sure there weren't any more treats, Snow White went back to her corner of the shelter. Soon she dropped her head and fell back to sleep.

But Acorn stayed wide-awake and as close to Anna as he could get. "Acorn, I do terrible in school. Sometimes I can get a good grade by doing oral reports or artwork instead of essays. But even with Pam and

Lulu helping me I don't pass my tests. I can't read good. I know I'm mixing up some of my letters and words. And it's getting harder and harder to fool people about that. Sometimes I can't even read the questions on a test."

Acorn whinnied softly as if to say, "I don't understand. Why are you crying?"

"Oh, Acorn," she sobbed, "I don't want to lose you. And I don't want you to lose me." She put her arms around his neck and hugged him. "I don't care if you never, ever jump. I don't care that you decide when to go and when to stop. I don't even care anymore why you behave the way you do. I just don't want to lose you. And I don't want you to have to go live with another mean kid like Tommy Rand."

She wiped her tears and opened the folder with the lists of spelling words. Acorn stayed right beside her as she copied the letters of the spelling words over and over.

Anna's Report Card

Monday, five minutes before the end of the school day, Mr. Livingston stood at the front of the room with a pile of envelopes in his hands. "Come up for your report cards when I call your name," he directed. "We'll go alphabetically by last name."

Anna's heart was pounding in her throat. She was praying, Please, please let my marks go up.

"Crandal, Pam," was the first Pony Pal to receive her report card. Anna knew that Pam would get all A's. Like always. And that her parents would take her out to dinner to celebrate. Like always.

Three names later Mr. Livingston called out, "Harley, Anna." As Anna walked to the front of the room she thought she could see that Mr. Livingston was disappointed in her.

She managed to whisper, "Thank you," as he placed the envelope in her opened hand.

Walking back to her desk she could feel that there was more than the thin report card in the envelope. She knew from past experience what a thick report card envelope meant. It was a sure sign she had failed. Inside her report card there would be a letter to her parents. The letter would ask them to set up a meeting with Mr. Livingston.

A few minutes later school was out. The Pony Pals headed toward Main Street together.

When they were out of earshot of other kids, Lulu said, "Anna, you have to open it sometime."

Pam tried to sound optimistic. "Maybe the letter is to your mother asking her to cater something."

"Yeah," Lulu agreed. "Or to your dad about doing a building job for Mr. Livingston. It doesn't have to be about you."

Anna didn't say anything.

Finally, when they were in Lulu's grandmother's kitchen getting a snack, Anna let Lulu open the envelope and look at her report card.

"You were right," Lulu told Anna sadly.

Pam looked over Lulu's shoulder to see Anna's grades. "We've got to talk to your parents ourselves. We can't let them take Acorn away from you."

"We didn't have enough time to help you," Lulu complained. "We'll tell your mother that from now on we'll study together every — "

Anna interrupted her. "Don't you understand? It won't make any difference." She took the report card from Lulu and finally looked at it. She got a C in social studies,

C — in science, D in math, and D in English. The same grades as last time. "I didn't improve in one subject," she said sadly. "And my parents said if I didn't get better grades I couldn't keep Acorn. They never, ever go back on their word."

"But look, you got an A in art," Pam told Anna. "And Mr. Livingston wrote 'Lively participant in class discussions, eager to learn' next to your social studies grade."

"And you had perfect attendance," Lulu said. "Those things should count for something."

That evening, Anna waited until her brother and sister had left for a high school basketball game before showing her parents her report card. Anna was nervous when they sat around the kitchen table to talk about her grades.

"Well, it's settled," her father said. "The pony goes back to Reggie Olson."

Anna had promised herself she wouldn't cry. But still she burst into tears.

"Now, now, Anna," her mother said, "maybe in a couple years you can get another pony. Or a horse."

"It's partly our fault," her father said. "We thought having the pony would motivate you to work harder at school. But I can see now it's been too much."

Her mother reached over and took her hand. "Anna, sweetie, please stop crying. That won't help. I bet Pam and Lulu will be very generous about letting you ride their ponies. After all, Snow White is right in your own backyard."

"I'm not crying for myself," Anna said. "I'm crying for Acorn."

"But why?" her mother asked. "I'm sure another family will take very good care of Acorn."

"Besides," her father said with a little smile, "that pony knows how to take care of himself."

Her mother added, "Remember, we're only doing this for your own good."

"Nobody understands," Anna sobbed.

"It's awful for Acorn and it's awful for me."

She shoved her chair back from the table, jumped up, and ran out the back door to find her pony.

That night Anna dreamt that she went to Mr. Olson's farm to see Acorn. Mr. Olson told her that he had sold Acorn to Tommy Rand. He handed her a piece of paper with Tommy Rand's address. But Anna couldn't read the address. All the letters on the paper and on the street signs looked jumbled to her. She ran all over Wiggins looking for help. But no one could help her. Anna woke up in the middle of the night crying and out of breath.

On the Run

The next morning, as Anna and Lulu were putting out fresh hay for their ponies, Anna pretended to cough four times. "I have a cold," she told Lulu. "My mother said I should stay home from school today."

"Don't worry," Lulu said. "Pam and I will come visit you after school. We've got to figure out a way for you to keep Acorn."

"It's no use," Anna told her. "My parents aren't going to change their minds."

Back in the house, Anna packed up her book bag and acted as if she were going to school. When she opened the front door to leave, she heard her father say to her mother, "I think Anna's accepted that the pony has to go."

Instead of walking to school, Anna snuck into her backyard and hid in the bushes along the edge of the paddock. Acorn came galloping over to greet her. She whispered to her pony, "I'm going to spend all day with you."

Anna watched her house. First, she saw her brother and sister get on the school bus that would take them to Eleanor Roosevelt Regional High. Next, her father backed out of the driveway in his red pickup truck. Finally, Anna saw her mother walk down Main Street toward her diner. Now that she was sure her family was gone, Anna snuck back into the house and packed up some water and food. She left plenty of room in her saddlebag for Acorn's favorite oats.

Back in the paddock she prepared Acorn for a ride. While she worked, Snow White stood by watching. When Anna led Acorn to the gate at the beginning of Pony Pal Trail, Snow White walked along beside them. Finally, Anna and Acorn were on the trail side of the gate. Snow White remained on the paddock side. Anna mounted Acorn and said, "Let's go."

Acorn stood still.

"What's wrong?" Anna asked. "You like to go on Pony Pal Trail."

Snow White whinnied. Acorn whinnied back. And Anna realized that Acorn didn't want to leave his friend. She felt sad. How many times had Acorn been separated from people and animals that he'd been attached to? He'd had eight different homes in twelve years. Now it would be nine. And it was her fault.

Anna looked behind them to be sure Snow White was all right. The pony was gaily galloping around the paddock.

"Come on, Acorn," Anna said. "We're going for a ride."

Acorn didn't move.

Anna squeezed her legs against his sides.

"Please, Acorn," she said, "don't do this to me now." But Acorn still didn't move.

Anna remembered what Mrs. Crandal told her about riding a pony who'd developed bad habits. "You're the one in charge," she'd said. "If you let Acorn know that, he will work with you. Then you can think through him and the two of you will move as one. But if the pony's in charge, you can't work together. It's not good for you. And it's not good for the pony."

So Anna focused on telling Acorn what she wanted him to do. She told him with her whole body, with her mind, and a tap of her heels against the pony's sides. And for the first time she really meant it.

Acorn understood Anna's message and moved forward. Anna and her pony moved as one. Riding on Acorn was great fun for Anna. And, because she would lose Acorn soon, riding him also made her sad.

When they'd covered about half of Pony Pal Trail, Anna said, "Acorn, you really are the most perfect pony. We're riding better than we ever have. And today you're going to jump with me, too."

Anna knew that if she went to the Crandals to jump, Dr. or Mrs. Crandal would be sure to see her. They would want to know why she wasn't in school. There was only one place for her to go to jump with Acorn.

Anna used the reins to tell Acorn that she wanted to turn left onto the Wiggins estate. And they did. Remembering the *No Trespassing* signs and the Wiggins Witch, she thought, I won't go far. Just to the two fields with the low stone wall between them. That will be perfect for jumping.

Minutes later she was directing Acorn into the open field. She checked both sides of the low stone wall to be sure the ground was free of snow and rocks. Then she trotted Acorn a good distance away. She moved him into a canter toward the low wall. She held the reins firmly, but gave Acorn the room to go forward. She concentrated all her thoughts on going over the wall. And just like that — they flew over it. When they landed, Acorn whinnied with delight.

Anna leaned over and stroked Acorn's neck. "Good pony," she cooed.

They were getting ready for their third jump when Anna saw something moving in the woods beyond the field. In a second she saw more clearly. It was a rider in red on a black horse. The Wiggins Witch! Anna turned Acorn around. They had to get out of there.

"Hey!" the rider's voice called out.

Anna squeezed her legs against Acorn's sides. "Go," Anna ordered. They rode like the wind across the open field. Before Anna and Acorn reached the middle of the field Anna heard the pounding of hooves behind her. The sound grew louder and louder as the hooves came closer and closer.

A big black horse pulled up alongside Acorn. "Stop!" a sharp voice ordered.

It *was* the Wiggins Witch.

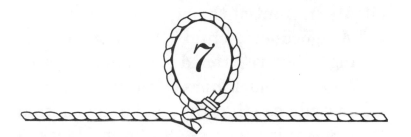

In the Wiggins Mansion

Anna had no intention of stopping. She wanted to get away from the woman in red. But Acorn, curious about the horse who'd come up alongside him, suddenly stopped. Anna pitched forward, almost over her pony's head, then fell back in the saddle. She looked up to see the Wiggins Witch turning her horse sharply around to face her and Acorn.

"I'm sorry," Anna stuttered breathlessly. "I promise I'll never come here again."

The big black horse pranced around excitedly in front of them.

"My goodness, child," the woman was saying. "I've frightened you. I'm so sorry."

When the black horse finally stood still, Anna could see that the woman had a kind face. She didn't look at all like she'd locked herself indoors for twenty-seven years with twenty-seven cats and no toothbrush.

"I was so surprised to see a child out here," she said. "At first I thought you were one of those hunters. They've been a terrible nuisance. Then I saw it was a child and a pony and I was — well — quite surprised. Are you all right?"

Anna nodded.

The black horse, which was twice as big as Acorn, bent its head to sniff Acorn's breath. Acorn sniffed back.

"Your pony is very dear," the woman said. "A pony is a wonderful thing to have. Do you know I still have my childhood pony? His name is Winston."

With that, Anna started to cry. The

woman looked sad. "Why, what's wrong?" she asked. "I'm sorry if I've frightened you. Is that why you're crying?"

Anna shook her head no. Now that she heard the woman's kind voice she was no longer afraid of her. What made her cry was the thought that she couldn't keep Acorn forever like the woman had kept *her* pony.

"Come," the woman directed. "Let's walk our horses around the field. The walk will do them good after our chase. We'll go side by side. If you want to tell me why you're crying, that's fine. If you don't, that's fine, too."

The smooth motion of Acorn's walk under her calmed Anna down. For the first half turn around the field they didn't speak. Finally, the woman broke the silence by saying, "Seeing you on your pony is bringing back such happy memories of my rides on Winston in these very fields. You know, you're never too old for a pony. I still go out with Winston. I harness him to a cart and drive him. When there's enough snow I

drive him with a sleigh. It's all great fun. And a pony makes a good stablemate if you get a riding horse as I did." She looked over and smiled at Anna. "By the way," she said, "my name is Wilhelmina Wiggins. But my friends call me Willie. And my horse is called Picasso."

Anna smiled back. "My name is Anna Harley," she said. "And this is Acorn. But I can't keep him the way you kept your pony."

While they took a second turn around the big field Anna told Wilhelmina Wiggins her whole sad story.

After hearing the story Ms. Wiggins said, "Our horses need a rest and something to drink. You and I could use the same. Come up to the house with me and we'll take care of all of us."

At the Wiggins' stables they gave their horses water and hay. Then they led them to the paddocks. Picasso joined Winston, and Acorn was put out in an adjoining paddock. The old gray Shetland and Acorn ran right up to the fence that separated them and whinnied friendly greetings. Picasso pranced about proudly as if to say, "I knew you two would get along."

As Anna and Ms. Wiggins walked toward the mansion, Anna asked, "Do you really live here all alone?"

"Yes, indeed," Ms. Wiggins answered. "I admit it's a lot of house for one person." She opened the front door. "Come on in."

Anna stepped into an entranceway as big as her living room at home. Facing her was a winding pink marble staircase. A painting hanging on the wall caught Anna's eye. It was the biggest, most beautiful painting she'd ever seen. Anna knew right away that the picture was a summer view of the fields where she and Ms. Wiggins had just been riding. Anna also recognized the black horse and gray pony that were galloping across the painted field.

She was breathless as she stared into the painting. It looked both real and unreal at the same time. Anna knew she'd never mistake the painting for a photograph. But she could still imagine herself walking right into the picture. Like in the most wonderful dream.

Ms. Wiggins stood beside her. "You like my painting?"

Anna whispered, "It's beautiful."

"One of the reasons I keep this place is because I love drawing and painting the landscape so much."

"I like to draw," Anna said. "But you're a real artist."

Ms. Wiggins laughed. "I have a feeling that you're a 'real' artist, too, Anna," she said. "While I start lunch, why don't you call your parents and tell them where you are?" She pointed to a low cabinet to her left. "There's a telephone over there."

Anna answered shyly, "They think I'm at school. I cut today."

"I see," Ms. Wiggins said thoughtfully. "I guess you'd rather deal with that later then."

Anna nodded.

As she followed Ms. Wiggins into the kitchen, Anna wondered how her parents would punish her for skipping school. What difference does it make? she thought. They've already given me the worst possible punishment. They are taking away Acorn.

More Visitors

The big kitchen windows gave Anna and Ms. Wiggins a good view of the two ponies and Picasso. Anna was glad to be eating Ms. Wiggins's delicious soup in the warm kitchen. And she liked talking to Ms. Wiggins.

Ms. Wiggins told Anna that she hadn't been a good student, either. "I had an impossible time with spelling," Ms. Wiggins said. "Even now I make spelling mistakes."

"Same with me," Anna said.

Then Ms. Wiggins asked Anna a lot of

questions about how she learned and how she solved problems. Ms. Wiggins listened thoughtfully to Anna's answers. "Anna, I think that you are dyslexic, just like me," she said. "That means you're very smart, but you reverse or rearrange letters."

"How come you know all this stuff and my teachers don't?" Anna asked.

"You're probably so clever that you've fooled them into thinking you can read better than you do," Ms. Wiggins answered.

"I haven't fooled Mr. Livingston," Anna said. "The work in fifth grade is a lot harder than the other grades."

"A good tutor would be a great help to you," Ms. Wiggins said. "Though I don't see how taking your pony away will help."

"That's just going to make me sad," Anna said.

After cookies and milk for dessert, Ms. Wiggins led Anna up two flights of the winding marble staircase, down a hall, and into a large room with windows on the ceiling.

Anna loved the room immediately.

"This is my art studio," Ms. Wiggins said.

Anna slowly walked around the studio. There was so much that interested her she didn't know where to go first. At one end of the room there were two easels with large unfinished landscape paintings. On a wooden table she saw neat rows of oil paint tubes and a bunch of paintbrushes of all sizes standing like bouquets in old jars. Paintings and drawings of the Wiggins estate were everywhere.

Anna thought that Ms. Wiggins was the luckiest person. She could paint and draw whenever she wanted. She had two beautiful horses and probably never had to remember the multiplication tables.

"If I'm not up here," Ms. Wiggins told Anna, "I'm usually outside with the animals."

"That's what I want to do when I grow up," Anna said. "Paint and have horses."

"I hope you can," Ms. Wiggins told her. "But for now I wish you could get your

teachers and parents to understand your difficulty with schoolwork. Have you ever talked to them the way you talked to me? You know, explaining how you learn and what your problems are?"

"I only told Acorn," Anna said.

"I think you should try hard to explain the situation to your parents and your teachers," Ms. Wiggins said.

Ms. Wiggins walked towards the window and looked out. "My goodness!" she exclaimed. "More children on ponies are coming this way. It's turning out to be a very social day."

Anna ran to her side. Through the window she saw her Pony Pals galloping toward Wiggins mansion.

"I'd bet you know those girls," Ms. Wiggins said.

"We're all best friends," Anna told her. "They must be looking for me."

Ms. Wiggins smiled. "Well," she said, "I suppose we should invite them in."

As they ran down the curving staircase,

Anna thought how smart and brave her friends were to trail her to the Wiggins mansion. And how frightened they must be of Ms. Wiggins. So when Ms. Wiggins opened the door, Anna blurted out, "It's okay. She's nice."

Pam and Lulu knew what Anna said was true because Ms. Wiggins had a warm and friendly smile.

Soon there were two more ponies in the paddocks outside the kitchen window. And two more girls around the kitchen table eating cookies and drinking milk.

Pam and Lulu explained what happened after school. They went to Anna's house to see how she was feeling and there was no one there. Then they went out back and saw that Acorn wasn't in the paddock.

"We were afraid he'd already gone back to Mr. Olson's," Pam said. "Then we saw all the hoofprints and footprints in the patches of snow leading to the trail; we knew you'd gone out with Acorn."

"Did you tell my parents?" Anna asked fearfully.

"Oh, no," Lulu exclaimed. "We thought you ran away. We wanted to find you and bring you back before they found out. We tracked you by following Acorn's hoofprints.

Pam grinned at Anna. "Acorn finally jumped with you didn't he?"

"Yup," Anna beamed. "Twice."

"We figured that out, too," Lulu told her. "But we were real scared when we saw there were two different sets of hoofprints."

"Did you think some mean, bad person had kidnapped her?" Ms. Wiggins asked.

The three girls sheepishly smiled at one another. "Sort of," Lulu admitted.

After Anna and Ms. Wiggins congratulated Pam and Lulu on their detective work, Ms. Wiggins wanted to know all about the girls and their families. Each girl told her where she lived and where her parents worked.

Ms. Wiggins said that she knew Pam's father because he was her veterinarian. She also knew Anna's mother because they had gone to Wiggins Elementary together. "And I drop by her diner once in awhile," she told Anna, "for a little chat and one of her chocolate brownies."

But of all the parents, Ms. Wiggins was most interested in Lulu's father. "He travels all over the world studying wildlife and writes about it," Lulu explained. "Sometimes I go with him. But not this time. He's in the Amazon jungle and I'd miss too much school. That's why I'm staying with my grandmother this year. She has a beauty shop on Main Street."

"When I wore my hair short, I used to visit your grandmother's salon more often," Ms. Wiggins said.

"I like your hair just the way it is now," Anna told her.

The other girls agreed that Ms. Wiggins's long black hair looked nice.

Before they left, Ms. Wiggins told Pam

and Lulu that she thought that Anna was dyslexic and explained what that meant. "I bet you three girls can work together to help her keep Acorn." Ms. Wiggins smiled.

"We'll try our best," Lulu said.

"We've solved lots of problems together," Pam added.

When the Pony Pals were back on their own trail it was time for Anna and Lulu to say good-bye to Pam.

"Ms. Wiggins gave us an important clue about why you have trouble with school-work," Pam said. "Now it's up to us to do something about it. Tomorrow morning let's meet before school starts and come up with a plan."

"Each of us should write out an idea of how Anna can keep Acorn," Lulu added.

The Pony Pals decided to meet the next day at 8:15 when the school building opened for early students.

But that afternoon, as Anna rode Acorn home along the trail, she wondered if her problems weren't too big for the Pony Pals.

Three Ideas Too Late

The next morning at 8:15 the custodian opened the doors to Wiggins Elementary. The Pony Pals went in and walked down the hall together.

"Did you get into trouble for cutting school?" Pam asked Anna.

"Yeah," she answered. "My mom found out when she called Mr. Livingston to make an appointment to talk about me." Anna remembered the sad look on her mother's face. "And my dad said I cut because of

Acorn. He said that it just proves I shouldn't have a pony."

"Don't worry," Pam told her. "We're going to help you."

The girls put their coats in their lockers, sat down on the floor, and took out their notebooks.

"Okay," Lulu said. "Who's going first? How about you, Pam?"

Pam read:

Tell Mr. Livingston that we think Anna is dyslexic and that he should give her a special test. Also, get him to tell Anna's parents all about dyslexia.

"That's perfect," Lulu said. "And all three of us should talk to him, not just Anna."

"Here's my idea," Anna said. "It's connected to Pam's."

SPECSHEL TUDOR 4 ME +

"I don't know how to spell, 'special tutor,' "
Anna said.

"But look how great you draw," Pam exclaimed. "I couldn't do that. That's what
Ms. Wiggins meant by, 'Different brains
work in different ways.' "

"Just the same," Anna said, "I want to
be able to read and spell better. And getting
extra homework isn't enough help. Ms.
Wiggins said I need a tutor. I wouldn't mind
studying a lot if I could keep Acorn."

"That's where my idea comes in," Lulu
said. She read from her notebook:

I will do Anna's pony chores so she has
more time to study. It's only fair because
I've been boarding Snow White at the
Harleys' for free.

174

Anna smiled at Lulu. "Thanks," she said, "but only if I really don't have time to do the chores myself."

"That's a great idea, Lulu," Pam said.

Anna agreed. "My parents are always saying that doing Acorn's chores takes up too much of my time. But if Lulu's doing the work, they can't use that as an excuse for taking him away from me."

The Pony Pals decided to put Pam's plan into action first. They rushed off to their classroom to talk to Mr. Livingston before the school day began.

The three girls told Mr. Livingston that they thought Anna was dyslexic. He said that he thought the same thing when he analyzed Anna's scores on the standardized reading tests. "That's why I've asked your parents to meet with me," he told Anna. "I need their permission to have you tested. If you're dyslexic, we'll have no trouble getting a specialist to work with you a couple of afternoons a week after school."

He leaned forward over his desk and spoke in his most serious teacher voice. "But, Anna, you're going to have to put in some hard work."

"I will," Anna said, "I promise. I want to do better in school. But I want to be able to keep my pony, too."

Mr. Livingston said that all he could do was explain what dyslexia was to Anna's parents and arrange for extra help.

"Can't you tell them that it's not her fault that she's not getting good grades?" Pam pleaded.

"Absolutely," he said. He looked down at his appointment book. "I'm seeing them Friday morning before school."

The warning bell rang signaling that kids in the hall should go to their homerooms. Now the other kids would be coming into the room.

"Mr. Livingston," Lulu said, "Friday is two days away. You've got to talk to Anna's parents before then. Or Anna might lose Acorn. Please, please, please."

"Couldn't you call them up or something?" Pam asked.

"The sooner the better," Anna added.

Now there were twenty other kids in the room. They were talking to one another and yelling good morning to Mr. Livingston.

"I'll see what I can do," Mr. Livingston said. "Now go to your places."

Before the Pony Pals separated to go to their seats, they exchanged smiles. Their first idea had worked out great.

After school that day the Pony Pals headed over to Anna's house. Their next step was to tell Mrs. Harley all about what Ms. Wiggins and what Mr. Livingston said about dyslexia.

As they ran down Main Street toward Anna's house, Pam said, "Lulu, don't forget to tell Anna's mother how you'll do a lot of the chores for Acorn."

They ran up the outside stairs to the back door. Pam got there first. "Anna," she said, "the door's locked. Is this one of the afternoons your mom works at the diner?"

Anna couldn't answer. She was standing on the landing staring out at the pony paddock. For a few seconds she didn't say anything.

When she finally spoke it was in a low whisper. "Acorn's gone."

Pam and Lulu could see in a glance that Snow White was alone in the backyard paddock.

Anna had tears running down her cheeks. "They didn't even let me say goodbye."

Where's Acorn?

The Pony Pals went out to the paddock to be absolutely, positively sure that Acorn wasn't there.

As they climbed through the fence rails into the small field, Lulu said, "Maybe he squeezed in behind the shelter. Some animals can make themselves real small."

"But not ponies," Pam commented.

Snow White galloped over to them and whinnied. Anna thought she sounded upset. "Maybe Acorn's hurt," she told her friends.

The Pony Pals looked around the bushes and trees along the inside edges of the paddock. And they checked behind the shelter. Snow White followed them everywhere. But there was only one pony in Acorn's paddock. And it wasn't Acorn. They all knew he'd been given back.

Snow White whinnied again.

"She's telling us she misses Acorn," Anna said quietly.

Pam and Lulu each put an arm around Anna's shoulders. Pam told her, "When we tell your parents about the dyslexia thing maybe they'll let you buy Acorn after all."

"Let's go to the diner and see if your mom's there. Okay?" Lulu said.

Anna nodded. She was feeling so sad she couldn't talk. Even to her best friends.

"Don't give up hope, Anna," Lulu said. "We'll get him back."

Through the front window of Off-Main Diner, Anna saw her mother walking to the back booth with two cups of coffee. "She's there," she told the others. Now she's sitting down with whoever's in that booth."

Pam cautioned, "Okay, guys, no matter what happens, we must stay calm. It's hard enough to explain this dyslexia stuff. Everybody agree?"

Lulu and Pam looked at Anna. Anna nodded. "I promise I won't cry." She paused before adding, "Unless I think it'll help."

The three Pony Pals were about to walk into the diner, when Pam motioned them to duck and said, "Quick, hide.

"I don't think she saw us," Pam whispered as they huddled down under the diner window.

"Who?" Lulu and Anna asked.

"Ms. Wiggins," Pam said. "That's who. She's the one in the booth."

"So why didn't we go in?" Lulu asked. "She's nice. She's on our side."

"That's exactly why," Pam advised. "Maybe she came to talk to your mother about you, Anna. We have to give her plenty of time to explain about dyslexia."

The girls took turns sneaking looks in through the diner window.

During Pam's turn they learned that Anna's mother got a telephone call.

During Anna's turn they learned that Ms. Wiggins and Anna's mother went to the counter to get brownies. And now they were sitting at the counter.

During her turn Lulu said, "They're laughing."

"It's time to make our move," Pam said.

The Pony Pals walked into the diner.

Anna's mother saw them first. "Well," she said with a laugh, "look what the cat dragged in."

Ms. Wiggins smiled at the girls, too. She said, "Anna, I've been telling your mother — "

But she didn't finish the sentence because Anna wailed, "Mommy, how could you send Acorn away? I didn't even get to say good-bye. . . ."

The cook looked out from the kitchen to find out what was going on.

The only sound in the diner was Anna's tearful voice asking, "Don't you know how much I love him?"

"It was Mr. Olson's idea to come after Acorn today," Anna's mother said. "Your father and I thought it might be easier on you. I left you a note in the kitchen explaining everything."

"We didn't go into the house," Pam told Mrs. Harley. Then she added quickly, "Mr. Livingston thinks Anna is dyslexic. Ms. Wiggins does, too."

"That's what Willie and I've been talking about," Anna's mother told the girls.

Lulu jumped in with her idea. "If you buy Acorn for Anna, I promise to do her afternoon chores in the paddock. That way she'll have lots of time to study. It'll be my way of paying for Snow White to stay there. I don't mind at all. It's only fair."

"Mr. Livingston said Anna can have a special tutor after school. For free," Pam added.

Anna listened to all of this and thought,

I have wonderful friends. Now if I could only get my pony back. . . .

She walked over to her mother. "I'm sorry I yelled," she said. "And I'm sorry I'm stupid."

Pam, Lulu, Ms. Wiggins, and Anna's mother shouted in unison, *"You're not stupid!"*

They all laughed. All except Anna. She had only one thing on her mind. And it wasn't a laughing matter. That's why she was still crying.

"Maybe you'd like to hear what your father and I were just talking about on the phone. Do you think you could stop crying and listen?"

Anna nodded and looked up at her mother.

"Mr. Livingston called your father at the shop a little while ago. He basically said the same thing Willie just told me. About this dyslexia business. Mr. Livingston also feels that taking away Acorn is too much like a punishment for something that hasn't been your fault. So we've decided to buy Acorn for — "

The Pony Pals didn't hear the rest of the sentence because they were jumping up and down with hoots and hollers and giving each other high fives.

Then they stopped suddenly. They'd all had the same thought at the same time.

Lulu was the first to put it into words. "Mr. Olson said he has someone else who wanted Acorn."

"That must be why he took him back right away," Pam said.

"Oh, no," Anna said. "Those other people could be picking up Acorn right now!"

A Ride with Winston

Two truck drivers walked into Off-Main Diner.

Mrs. Harley told Ms. Wiggins and the girls, "I've got to get back to work." She got off the stool and went up to meet the men.

Anna followed Mrs. Harley as she led the customers to a booth. She was pleading with her mother, "But, Mom, you've got to sign the papers and give me a check. I have to get to Olson's before somebody else takes Acorn. We've got to hurry."

"We're in a bit of a hurry ourselves,

ma'am," one of the customers told Mrs. Harley.

Pam came over to the booth. "I'll take their order, Mrs. Harley," Pam said. Then she told the men, "Our specials today are lasagna or meatloaf with mashed potatoes."

Lulu came to the booth and handed out menus. "I'll be right back with water and rolls," she said.

Mrs. Harley was smiling as she handed Pam her pad and pencil. "Pam will take your order," she said to her customers.

Two more customers were walking through the front door. Lulu ran up to greet them and to ask them where they'd like to sit.

As Anna followed her mother back to the counter she slipped off her backpack and unzipped it. "I have the sale papers right here," she told her mother. She pulled out the page that Mr. Olson had given her and put it on the counter. "Just sign it and make out a check. Okay?"

Ms. Wiggins handed Mrs. Harley a pen.

As her mother carefully read the page Anna remembered her nightmare. What if Mr. Olson already sold Acorn to someone else?

Finally her mother signed the document and made out a check. "Now," she said, "I'd better get back to work. How will you get over to Olson's farm?"

"I can drive her," Ms. Wiggins offered.

"Do you know where it is?" Anna asked.

"I do," Ms. Wiggins answered.

Mrs. Harley went back to her customers and Pam and Lulu followed Ms. Wiggins and Anna. When they were outside, Ms. Wiggins turned to them and said, "I'm afraid I only have room for Anna." She smiled at Anna, "I'm glad you're small."

The Pony Pals exchanged questioning glances. How could Ms. Wiggins have a car so small that Anna's size would make a difference? Pam and Lulu were so curious about this situation that they walked around to the parking lot with Anna.

A pony's neigh greeted them. There, in the fenced-in area behind the parking lot, the Pony Pals saw Ms. Wiggins's pony, Winston. The pony cart stood in a parking space near two big trucks.

"Don't worry," Ms. Wiggins told Anna as she hitched Winston to the cart. "He'll get you there in a hurry. Winston can put on the steam when I ask him to. Besides, I know an old trail that's a shortcut to Olson's."

Anna enjoyed the pony cart ride so much that for a few minutes she forgot that they might be too late to get her own pony back. And when Ms. Wiggins let her take the reins on an easy part of the trail, Anna imagined herself years from now with Acorn pulling her in a cart.

When they got to Olson's, Ms. Wiggins drove Winston right past the parking area and over the field toward the barn. She told

Anna, "This is one of the great advantages of a pony and cart. You don't always need a road."

But Anna wasn't paying much attention to what Ms. Wiggins was saying. She was checking out the paddocks to see if Acorn was among Olson's dozen or so horses and ponies.

"He's not here," she told Ms. Wiggins.

"Well, maybe he's in the barn," Ms. Wiggins said. "Look, there's Reggie Olson."

Anna saw he was standing in front of the barn. He waved at them and called out, "Hey, hey, Willie. You ready to sell me that old pony?"

When they reached Mr. Olson, Ms. Wiggins told Winston, "Whoa." She smiled at Mr. Olson. "Reggie, you know I'll never sell Winston. I've brought my young friend over to buy her pony."

Mr. Olson slapped his thigh happily and exclaimed, "The Harley girl! I knew you'd be wanting something bigger than that Shetland. And lucky for you, young lady, that I still have the Morgan."

Anna jumped out of the cart. "I don't want another horse. I want Acorn back." She looked around desperately. "Where is he?"

"I have another family that wants to buy him," Mr. Olson said.

Anna held up the paper and said, "My mother signed it." She held up the check. "And here's the money. I have to have Acorn," she said with determination. "He can't go to someone else."

"Reggie, Anna and Acorn are quite a pair," Ms. Wiggins said. "You can find another pony for your customer."

Mr. Olson took the document and check from Anna. She held her breath while he studied them.

"Well," Mr. Olson said slowly, "the other folks haven't signed anything. To be perfectly honest, they haven't even seen Acorn yet."

He nodded over his shoulder toward the barn. "He's in there," Mr. Olson said.

"Thank you. Oh, thank you so much," Anna said. Then she ran into the barn. She passed several stalls of horses and ponies before she found her pony. "Acorn, Acorn," she called out happily.

Acorn was so glad to see her that he stopped eating. Anna opened the stall door and went in to give him a hug.

Mr. Olson came up to the stall. "I can't trailer him back to your place until tomorrow," he said.

"I'll ride him back," Anna told him. "And I want the same saddle and everything."

A few minutes later Acorn was saddled up. Anna led him out of the barn and over to where Ms. Wiggins and Winston were waiting for her. "You lead the way back, Anna," Ms. Wiggins said as she climbed into the seat of her driving cart.

Anna mounted Acorn, found her stirrups, and took proper hold of the reins. Then she pressed her legs against her pony's sides. "Let's go Acorn," she said.

Acorn didn't move.

Anna remembered what Mrs. Crandal had taught her. She had to concentrate and tell Acorn what she wanted. She focused very hard and used her whole body and mind to tell Acorn what to do. And they moved forward.

As she trotted along the old trail on her pony Anna thought, I guess you and I are a lot alike, Acorn. To get along we've had to do things our own way. Now it's time for both of us to make some changes. You're already learning how to work with me. And I'm going to have to work with my tutor.

A minute later Anna laughed out loud. Acorn was hers for keeps. And now she knew that no matter how big she got, with a pony cart she could ride him forever. Just like Ms. Wiggins and Winston behind her.

Anna took a deep breath of the crisp winter air and looked between Acorn's ears at the path ahead. She couldn't wait to show this new trail to her Pony Pals.

A Pony in Trouble

For Ryan

The author thanks Dr. Kent Kay for medical consultation on this story.

Thanks also to Elvia Gignoux and Helen Perelman for their editorial assistance.

A Beautiful Morning

Pam Crandal woke up to her dog's loud bark. The family dog, Woolie, slept in the kitchen. Early in the morning when he was let out into the yard, his bark was Pam's wake-up call.

Pam got out of bed and looked out the window to the paddock below. Her chestnut-colored pony, Lightning, was standing under the big sugar maple tree. That's where the pony spent the night. Lightning was watching the dog dashing around the paddock. She neighed at Woolie as if to

say, "Good Morning. What's all the fuss about?"

Pam dressed and had a bowl of cereal before she went out to feed Lightning. When the pony saw Pam, she galloped toward her. By the time Pam opened the paddock gate, Lightning was there to greet her with a gentle nudge on the shoulder. Pam returned the greeting with a good-morning hug around the pony's neck.

"It's spring vacation," she told Lightning. "That means we'll be together all day long."

Pam gave Lightning fresh water to drink and some oats and hay. "Eat up," she told her pony. "We're going on a big trail ride today."

Pam left Lightning and went to the barn to do all her morning chores. Winter was finally over and a whole week of spring vacation lay ahead. She knew that her best friends, Anna Harley and Lulu Sanders, were doing their barn chores, too. When they were finished, Anna and Lulu would ride over to Pam's on their ponies, Acorn and Snow White. They'd take the mile-and-a-half path through the woods connecting Pam's house and Anna's house. The three friends called it Pony Pal Trail.

Pam was on her way out of the barn when she noticed a poster on her mother's barn-office door. She went up to the door to get a better look. WIGGINS HORSE SHOW, the poster announced.

Pam was reading the poster when she felt a hand on her shoulder. Pam jumped. She looked up to see her mother standing beside her.

"Sorry I scared you, honey," Mrs. Crandal said. "I thought you heard me come in." She pointed to the poster. "Didn't the poster for the horse show come out nice?"

"It looks great," Pam said.

"It's really a shame that you don't enter Lightning in horse shows," Mrs. Crandal said. "I picked her out especially because I knew she'd be a great show pony for you."

Pam remembered the day two years ago when her parents drove her to Echo Farm

202

to pick out a Connemara pony. She'd tried two other ponies before Mr. Echo brought over Lightning. In a few turns around the ring, Pam knew that Lightning was perfectly trained.

After that first ride, Pam studied Lightning's face. That's when she noticed that the white marking on the pony's forehead was shaped like an upside-down heart. She also noticed the alert, friendly look in Lightning's dark eyes.

To Pam, Lightning seemed to be saying, "Come on. Take me home. You know we belong together." That's when Pam knew that she and this pony were meant for each other.

Pam turned to her mother, "You didn't pick out Lightning, Mom. I did."

"That's true," her mother said. "But I made sure we only looked at ponies that had good potential for showing. I wish you'd let Lightning show off what she can do."

Competing in horse shows was something that Pam and her mother disagreed about a lot. Mrs. Crandal thought that being in a horse show was a big deal. As a riding teacher she worked hard preparing kids to be in horse shows. Pam felt that her mother was disappointed in her for not being in them. But she couldn't help it. She hated horse shows.

"I didn't pick out Lightning because she could win a bunch of ribbons," Pam said.

"Being in horse shows is more than winning ribbons," her mother said.

"Well, I just don't like them," Pam said.

"I'll bet your friends will want to be in the show," Mrs. Crandal said. "Snow White is such a good jumper. And I figured that Anna would be excited that the show is at Reggie Olson's farm where she bought Acorn."

Pam didn't tell her mother that she hadn't told her friends about the horse show. Instead she said, "None of us like horse shows. We're going trail riding all week."

Just then Pam heard the sound of horses'

hooves. Through the open barn door she could see Anna and Lulu galloping toward her on their ponies.

"Come quickly!" Anna shouted. "Something's wrong with Lightning."

Pam ran ahead of her mother and past her friends into the paddock. In a far corner she saw Lightning pawing the ground and kicking. Pam raced across the paddock toward her pony.

She knew something was terribly wrong.

The Mystery Illness

"What's wrong, Lightning?" Pam asked.

For a split second Lightning raised her head and looked at Pam. Pam saw pain and fear in her pony's eyes. It was a look that shouted "Help me." The moment passed and Lightning lowered her head again and tried to kick her own stomach.

Pam's father was a veterinarian who ran a clinic for large animals. So Pam had been around sick horses all her life. Now, for the first time, her *own* pony was the one in trouble.

Lulu and Anna rode up beside Pam.

"What's wrong with her?" Lulu asked.

"I think it's her stomach," Pam answered.

"Your mother's gone to get your father," Anna said.

Pam told Lightning, "Dad'll be here in a minute. He'll know what to do to help you."

Pam thought of what else had to be done. She told Lulu, "We'll need a halter and a lead rope."

"Okay," Lulu said. She turned Snow White around and cantered back toward the barn to get one.

Pam turned to Anna, "For now you'd better put Acorn in the other paddock. And Snow White, too, when Lulu comes back." Pam was relieved to see her father and mother rushing across the paddock.

A few minutes later, Pam's father told the Pony Pals what Pam had already guessed. "Lightning has colic," he said. Pam knew that colic was an upset stomach and problems in the intestines. She also knew that horses could die from colic.

"Ponies hardly ever throw up because of the way their stomachs are built," Pam said to Lulu.

"I know," Lulu said sadly.

Pam remembered the time she'd got food poisoning from spoiled mayonnaise at a picnic. It was the worst upset stomach she'd ever had. For a whole day she had terrible cramps. She threw up over and over again. What would have happened if she hadn't been able to get rid of what was making her sick?

"We worm her regularly," Dr. Crandal said, "so I don't think it's a parasite." He gave Lightning two shots. One was a pain-killer. The other was to help her digestion.

"What has she been eating?" Mrs. Crandal asked.

"Oats and hay," Pam told her mother.

"How much?" Dr. Crandal asked.

Pam cupped her hand and put it out. "A handful of oats. And two flakes of hay. Like always," she said.

"That shouldn't cause this trouble. Better check that hay to be sure it isn't moldy," he said.

Pam felt awful. Had she made her own pony sick?

"Let's get her to walk around a little," Dr. Crandal said.

While her father held Lightning's head, Pam quickly slipped on the halter. "We're going to help you," she told Lightning. Then, more to herself than the pony, she added, "Be brave."

"Now walk her," Dr. Crandal directed.

Pam attached the lead rope to the halter. Lulu and Anna stood on either side of Pam. Now Lightning could see all three Pony Pals.

"Come on Lightning," Anna cooed. "Come with us."

"You can do it," urged Lulu. "We're all here to help you get better."

"Trust me," Pam told her pony. "I wouldn't ask you to do anything that wasn't good for you."

She pulled on the rope. Lightning moved a few steps forward. Pam and Lulu walked backward as they continued their encouraging words. And the pony continued to walk.

Dr. Crandal watched Lightning a while longer. "You girls are doing fine here with her," he said. "Keep her walking. Then we'll see how she's doing when the painkiller wears off."

Dr. Crandal went back to the animal clinic. Mrs. Crandal and Anna went into the barn to check if the hay was moldy. That left Pam and Lulu to walk Lightning.

"Thanks for helping, Lulu," Pam said as they led Lightning in a slow circle around the paddock.

As they walked her pony, Pam thought about how lucky she was to have two great best friends — Anna and Lulu.

Of the three Pony Pals, Anna was the most artistic. She loved to draw and to paint, especially pictures of horses. Anna was dyslexic, so reading and writing were hard for her. But that didn't mean she wasn't smart. Pam and Anna had been best friends since the day they met in kindergarten. Anna's mother owned the only diner in Wiggins — Off-Main Diner — and her father was a carpenter. He'd built the Crandals' barn.

Lulu's dad used to spend summers in Wiggins when he was a kid. Now his mother — Lulu's grandmother — lived in Wiggins all the time. And while Lulu's father was working in the Amazon jungle, Lulu was living with her grandmother in the house right next door to Anna. Best of all, Acorn and Snow White shared a paddock behind Anna's house.

It made Pam sad to remember that Lulu's mother had died when Lulu was little. But Pam knew that Lulu was very close to her father. They both loved the outdoors and adventure. Lulu's father was a naturalist who wrote about animals. He traveled for his work and usually took Lulu with him.

For two years, Lulu and her dad lived in England. Their cottage was right near a horse farm. That's where Lulu had taken riding lessons. Lulu knew almost as much about horses as Pam did.

"Pam," Lulu said, "look what Snow White and Acorn are doing."

Pam looked up to see the two ponies walking along the fence that separated them from Lightning. They were staying as close as possible to their friend.

"They're worried about her and want to keep her company," Lulu said.

Anna ran across the paddock toward Pam and Lulu. "The hay's not moldy," she told them. "So that's not what made Lightning sick."

"I wish I knew what did it," Pam said. "Then maybe I could keep it from happening again."

"Your dad said sometimes horses get sick and you never know why," Lulu said. Lulu patted Lightning on the neck. "I think she's going to be all right."

Anna gave Lightning a kiss on the cheek. "I think so, too."

But Pam couldn't help thinking, What if Lightning doesn't get better?

Choosing a Color

An hour later, Pam's father came out to check on Lightning. "She'll be okay," he told the girls.

The Pony Pals exchanged smiles of relief.

"Just let her rest today. And give her warm mash for supper," he said.

When Dr. Crandal left, Pam told her friends, "You guys go ahead and do the trail ride without Lightning and me." She looked up at the bright blue sky. "It's a great day for a ride."

"No, we'll hang out here today," Anna said.

"And have our picnic with you," Lulu added.

"I've got brownies from Mom's diner," Anna told them, "for all of us."

Pam's mouth watered as she remembered the delicious taste of Off-Main Diner's famous brownies. She was feeling more like herself now that she knew her pony was going to be okay. And she was glad her friends were going to stay with her.

"Let's brush Lightning," Anna suggested. "It'll help her relax."

Lulu and Anna led Lightning close to the barn while Pam ran ahead to get a grooming box. A few minutes later, the pony was sighing contentedly as the three girls petted and brushed her.

"I didn't know there was going to be a horse show at Olson's," Lulu said.

"A show?" Anna asked excitedly.

"I saw a poster for it on Mrs. Crandal's door," Lulu said. "When I got the harness."

Anna put down the currycomb. "Show me, Lulu," she said.

Pam was surprised that Anna was so interested. As her friends headed into the barn, Lulu turned and asked, "You coming, Pam?"

"I saw it already," Pam answered.

Through the open barn door Pam listened to Anna and Lulu reading the poster and talking about the show. "There's a Short Stirrup Division," Anna said. "That's perfect for me and Acorn."

"And a Pony Hunter Division that'll have a lot of jumping over fences," Lulu said. "That's just what Rema wants me to compete in with Snow White."

Pam, running her fingers through Lightning's mane, remembered that Snow White wasn't really Lulu's pony. Lulu was only taking care of the pretty white pony until her real owner, Rema Baxter, got home from boarding school in June. Lulu had to write reports to Rema telling her everything about Snow White.

When Anna and Lulu came back outside, Pam said, "Aren't horse shows dumb? Who would want to be showing off in front of a lot of people when you could be trail riding?"

"The neat thing about this show is that it's at Olson's farm," Anna said. "We can ride there. We don't have to borrow a horse trailer or anything."

"Snow White's a good jumper, so maybe we'll win some ribbons," Lulu put in. "Rema would like that."

"Rema's the sort of person who counts every ribbon she's won," Anna said.

Pam put her arms around Lightning's neck and gave the pony a hug. "I wouldn't ask Lightning to be in a show just so I could have a prize."

"I've only been in horse shows in England," Lulu said. "They were lots of fun whether I won ribbons or not. Aren't they fun in America, too?"

"I think so," Anna told Lulu. "I was in shows when I took lessons from Pam's mom. But I've never been in a show with Acorn." Anna turned to Pam. "Don't you think Acorn would have fun being in a horse show?"

"Acorn thinks trail riding is fun. Like us," Pam answered.

"But if we were all in the show," said Anna, "we would make it fun. We could all use the same color to decorate our ponies."

"It'd be our Pony Pal color," Lulu said.

Anna put her arm around Pam's shoulder. "Please, say you'll do it."

"*You* be in the horse show with Lulu," Pam told Anna. "But count me out."

"Pam, the show won't be the same if we don't all do it," Lulu said.

"Maybe you'll change your mind," Anna said.

"I won't," Pam insisted.

They were all quiet for a minute. This was the first time they were planning to do something that split them up. Pam knew it was her fault. But she couldn't help it.

"Let's have lunch," Lulu said, breaking the silence.

They put out an old horse blanket near the paddock. While they ate their sandwiches, they talked about how scary it was to have a sick pony. Then they talked about how much fun it was to trail ride. No one mentioned the horse show until they were eating the brownies.

"I think it'll be neat to have a Pony Pal color for the horse show," Anna said. "We can even decorate our riding sticks with the color we pick."

"And get yarn to braid in our ponies' manes," Lulu added. She looked from Anna to Pam. "So what should our color be?"

Anna pointed to the sky. "How about that shade of blue?" she asked. Lulu and Pam looked up. "It's called periwinkle blue," Anna explained.

"Perfect," Lulu said. "What do you think, Pam?"

"It's a pretty color," Pam said.

"Do you think it should be the Pony Pal color?" Anna asked.

"Sure. Why not?" Pam said. "But I'm still not going to be in the horse show. So don't ask me again, okay?"

"I wasn't asking you to be in the show," Anna pointed out. "Just if you voted yes for the color."

"Yes, I vote yes for the color," Pam said. She hated that her friends were trying to get her to be in a horse show. They're acting just like my mother, she thought.

"Come on, Lulu, let's go get the program and prize list from Mrs. Crandal," Anna said.

After they left, Pam decided that Lightning was ready to go in the big paddock with the other ponies. Lightning whinnied happily when she saw she was going to be let out with Acorn and Snow White.

"You didn't like being separated from your friends, did you?" she said to her pony. She leaned her head against Lightning's neck and sighed. "I'm beginning to know how that feels."

Not Again!

Early the next morning, Pam woke up to her bark-alarm. She smiled when she heard Lightning's cheerful neigh.

When Pam went out to the paddock, Lightning ran over to her and nudged her shoulder like always. That was a good sign, too. And after a drink of water, Lightning ate every last bite of her breakfast. Another good sign.

Before eating her own breakfast, Pam telephoned Lulu to tell her the good news. "Lightning's all better," she said. "Dad said I can take her out on a trail ride to-day."

"Great," Lulu said. "Anna and I are practicing with your mother for the horse show this morning. But after we finish, we'll go trail riding."

When she got off the phone, Pam wondered what she'd do while her friends were practicing. Was she going to spend all of spring vacation waiting around for Lulu and Anna while they rode with her mother and her riding students?

A little later, as Pam was fixing a picnic lunch for the trail ride, she heard a frightened whinny. At first she thought it was an injured horse being brought into her father's clinic for surgery. But when she heard the whinny a second time, she knew it came from Lightning's paddock. Pam ran out the kitchen door. In the middle of the field, she saw her pony rolling on the ground in pain.

Pam's father gave Lightning two shots, just like the day before. But this time it took longer to get the pony walking.

"She's even sicker than she was yesterday," Pam said.

"This is the second time it's happened to her," Dr. Crandal said. "I don't like that."

"What's making her sick, Dad?" Pam asked.

"If I didn't know better," he said, "I'd say this pony's been overeating." He looked around the paddock. "But there's not enough grass here for her to overgraze."

A car pulled into the parking area next to the animal clinic. "I have to get back to the clinic," he said. "Come get me if there's an emergency."

Pam felt lonely and discouraged as she led her pony around the paddock. Finally she saw Anna and Lulu coming off Pony Pal Trail.

When her friends reached her, Pam told them what had happened. "You guys should go ahead and practice with Mom," she said. "There's nothing you can do to help."

"I can't practice jumping when Lightning is sick again and we don't know why," Lulu said.

"There has to be *something* we can do," Anna said. "Let's think hard."

Pam kicked the ground with her foot. "I went over everything with my dad already," she said. Pam was about to kick the grass again, but stopped herself. On the ground, new grass and plants were just beginning to grow. "What about poisonous plants?" she said.

"Where?" Anna asked.

"Maybe growing right here in this paddock," Pam answered. "New plants we haven't noticed yet. You stay with Lightning," she told her friends. "I'll be right back."

Pam ran to her mother's office where there was a whole bookcase of books about horses. It didn't take her long to find exactly what she was looking for.

Back in the paddock, she showed Anna and Lulu two pages with pictures of plants poisonous to horses. "We'll check every inch of the paddock," she told them. "If we find a plant that looks like any of these, we'll dig it up."

The girls crawled up and down the field on their hands and knees.

Half an hour later, they'd finished their search without finding one poisonous plant. They sat on the ground and leaned against the paddock fence to rest. Pam saw that Lightning was standing in her favorite spot under the sugar maple tree. Her head was drooping.

"Lightning doesn't seem like herself," she said.

"Getting sick two days in a row has made her weak," Dr. Crandal said.

The girls looked up to see Pam's dad standing behind them on the other side of the fence.

"What can we do for her?" Pam asked.

"If she's not better tomorrow I'll run some more tests," he said. "All you can do right now is keep an eye on her."

After he left, Lulu turned to Pam and Anna. "What your dad just said reminds me of something my dad's always saying."

"What?" Pam asked.

" 'If you want to know how an animal lives, you have to watch the animal twenty-four hours a day.' Once my dad and another guy followed a group of gorillas to do this article for a nature magazine. At night they took turns sleeping so one of them would always be watching the gorillas."

"Even when the gorillas were sleeping?" Anna asked.

"Yup," Lulu said.

"Are you saying we should watch Lightning every second for twenty-four hours?" Pam asked.

"Yup," Lulu repeated.

"That's a *great* idea, Lulu," Pam said. "Then I'd know if she's doing something that makes her sick."

"What about at night?" Anna asked. "Pam can't stay awake all night long."

"If we have a barn sleepover," Lulu said, "we could take turns."

Pam was happy that her friends were trying so hard to help Lightning. And she was happy that they and their ponies would be staying for a sleepover.

But Pam was still sad. What if the Pony Pals couldn't figure out what was making Lightning sick? What if tomorrow Lightning got sick again? Or worse?

Pony Watch

That evening the Pony Pals ate a picnic dinner on the big flat rock at the far edge of the paddock. From there they could see their ponies and keep a special watch over Lightning.

"We've watched Lightning for eight hours so far," Pam said. "And she hasn't done anything that would make her sick."

The rock was flat enough for the checkerboard, so that's what the girls did next. "Just be sure one of us is always looking

at Lightning," Pam reminded her fellow detectives.

At nine o'clock Dr. Crandal came out to check on Lightning. He told the girls that she was recovering very well. "But I'd still like to know what gave her colic," he said. He gave Pam a kiss good night and said to the Pony Pals, "You all get a good night's sleep." Woolie was sniffing at his legs. "Come on, fella," he said. "Time to go in."

"Woolie can sleep with us tonight," Pam said. The dog yapped excitedly, as if he understood that he wouldn't be sleeping alone in the kitchen.

When Dr. Crandal left, the Pony Pals and Woolie went into Mrs. Crandal's office in the barn. They'd chosen the office as their "post" because of the room's big window facing the paddock.

Pam put a small clock and a piece of paper on the desk. "Here's the overnight schedule," she said.

PONY WATCH

9:00 P.M.	12:00 midnight	Anna's turn
12:01 A.M.	3:00 A.M.	Lulu's turn
3:01 A.M.	6:00 A.M.	Pam's turn

"Wouldn't it be easier if we just put Lightning in a stall for the night?" Anna asked.

"Sleeping in the barn isn't what Lightning normally does," Lulu said. "We're not changing what she does. We're spying to see if she starts to do something that could make her sick."

"Besides," Pam added, "Lightning likes to sleep outdoors."

Anna sat on the desk and looked out the window. "You guys should go to sleep while I watch," she said.

Pam and Lulu laid out their sleeping bags and scrunched into them.

Pam watched Anna put on her Walkman headphones. Because Anna didn't read very well, she sometimes listened to

235

books on tape. During their all-night Pony Watch, the Pony Pals were going to take turns listening to *Black Beauty*, the famous novel by Anna Sewell. It was a perfect way to stay awake.

Pam could hear from Lulu's breathing that she was definitely asleep. So was Woolie, who was curled up between them. Pam was feeling pretty sleepy herself. She turned over and faced the wall.

By the moonlight, Pam could make out all the horse-show ribbons hanging there. To help her fall asleep she began to count them the way some people count sheep. One, two, three, four, five. . . . She got all the way to forty-nine before she closed her eyes. The next thing she knew, Lulu was waking her up.

Pam wiggled out of her sleeping bag, stepped over the sleeping dog, and went over to her mother's desk to take Lulu's place.

"Did you see anything?" Pam whispered.

"Lightning's been standing under the

236

tree sleeping the whole time," Lulu answered. "During Anna's watch, too." She handed Pam the Walkman and earphones. "*Black Beauty* is great. It made me cry."

For the next two and a half hours Pam stared at her own pony while listening to the sad, wonderful story of a horse. Just when things got better for Black Beauty, his life would change from good to bad.

Pam was watching the sun rising behind her own beautiful pony. Suddenly, Lightning woke up and ran across the paddock, out of sight. Pam pulled off the earphones and shouted, "Something's happening!"

She raced from the barn with Woolie at her heels. Behind her she could hear Anna and Lulu scrambling out of their sleeping bags.

As Pam bolted out of the barn, she saw that someone was at the paddock fence. Lightning was there, too. The person was holding a bag in one hand and offering Lightning something to eat with the other hand.

"Stop!" Pam screamed as she ran toward them. Woolie raced ahead and barked his loudest, fiercest bark.

Pam could see now that the person was a girl. The girl dropped the bag and jumped on her bike. Pam and Woolie chased her down Riddle Road, but the girl pedaled away faster than either of them could run. She turned the bend in the road and was out of sight.

When Anna and Lulu reached Riddle Road, Pam breathlessly told them, "Someone was feeding Lightning. Maybe poison."

Acorn and Snow White were at the fence with Lightning. The three ponies were sticking their noses under the fence. They wanted whatever that girl had dropped. Pam ran over and kicked the brown bag out of their reach.

The Pony Pals squatted around the bag.

"Don't touch it," Lulu warned. "We might mess up the girl's fingerprints. That's evidence."

Anna poked the bag with a stick so they could see inside.

"It's only some apples," Lulu said.

Pam's mother and father had come out to the paddock. "What's all the racket?" her father asked.

"What's going on?" her mother asked.

"We know why Lightning's been getting sick," Pam answered. "Someone's been feeding her poisoned apples."

The Racing Bike

"Maybe I should stay outside in case she comes back," Pam said, as she followed her parents and friends into the kitchen.

"She's not coming back so fast," Anna said. "You and Woolie really scared her."

Holding the bag by a corner, Pam dumped the apples onto the table.

"How could an apple be poisoned?" Lulu asked.

"Remember the story of Snow White?" Anna said. "One bite of an apple put her to sleep for about a million years."

"They smell like regular apples," Pam said.

Dr. Crandal studied them, too. He told the girls that while the apples were a little old, there was nothing about them that would make a pony sick.

"Unless," he said, "Lightning ate three or four apples in addition to her regular diet."

"If that girl fed Lightning apples yesterday and the day before, too," Pam said, "could that be what made her sick?"

"Most definitely," Dr. Crandal answered. "I'd say you girls solved the mystery of why Lightning is getting sick. She's been over-eating."

"Congratulations, girls," Mrs. Crandal said. "You probably saved Lightning's life."

The Pony Pals didn't hit high fives or congratulate one another the way they usually did. They were very quiet. Instead of feeling proud and happy, they were feeling frightened. Frightened at the thought of

241

how close Lightning had come to dying.

"Now we've got to make sure that girl never, ever, gets near Lightning," Pam whispered.

Mrs. Crandal handed Pam a pile of cereal bowls to put on the table. "During the day Lightning will be with you girls," Pam's mother said. "So she's safe for now. And maybe at night she should stay in the barn."

But what about when I have to go back to school? Pam thought. She had to find that girl.

"This morning let's get some of the winter coats off our ponies," Lulu said. "Then this afternoon we can go on a trail ride."

"Great idea, Lulu," Anna said. "And I'm going to trim Acorn's tail. He'll be so beautiful for the horse show."

"And don't forget, girls," Mrs. Crandal said, "there's a riding lesson for the show at ten." She turned to Pam. "Now that Lightning's better maybe you'll join us."

"No thanks," Pam said.

After breakfast the Pony Pals went out to the paddock and fed their ponies. Then they cleaned up Mrs. Crandal's office from the sleepover and did Pam's barn chores. Finally, they were ready for the big grooming session.

Their ponies loved to be groomed, so it was never a problem to keep them still. "Let's all do all three of them at the same time," Anna suggested. "I'll do manes and tails."

"And I'll use the shedding blade," Pam said.

"I'll follow you with the currycomb," Lulu added.

"Then we'll all do the final brushing," Anna said.

As the Pony Pals gave the ponies their six-hands grooming special, they talked about the mystery girl who had been feeding Lightning.

They agreed that for Lightning's safety

they had to find the girl. Pam needed to know for sure if she had fed Lightning before. "I want to be positively sure that overeating is what's making her sick," Pam said.

"And we should tell her to never, ever, do it again," Lulu added. "To Lightning or any other pony."

"How are we going to find her?" Anna asked.

"We have to remember everything we can about her," Lulu answered. "Especially you, Pam, because you saw her best."

"She's tall," Pam said. "Taller than any of us. So she's probably older than we are. She's probably Anna's sister's age. But not an adult. And I think I saw red hair sticking out from under her bike helmet."

"A redhead," Lulu said. "That should make her easier to find."

"And her bike is special," Pam recalled. "A fancy racing bike. It's black."

"A black racing bike," Anna said. "I think I've seen something like that around town."

"Where?" Pam asked.

"I don't know," Anna said. "It's just this feeling I have."

The five-year-old Crandal twins, Jack and Jill, came running across the paddock to where the Pony Pals were finishing Snow White's grooming. "Mom says — " Jack shouted.

"Mom says," Jill repeated when they reached the girls and their ponies.

Jack breathlessly completed the sentence, " — that it's time to practice for the horse show."

"Right," said Jill.

"We haven't finished grooming Lightning," Anna said.

"You guys go ahead," Pam said. "I'll finish her myself."

While Pam groomed her pony, she listened to the sounds coming from the out-

245

door rink where her best friends and her mother's students were riding. Pam remembered her first and only horse show. Everyone had expected her to do great because she was the teacher's daughter and had been riding since she was real little. But she did the worst of all her mother's students. She hadn't won any ribbons. It was nerve-racking and embarrassing to be in horse shows. How could anyone think it was fun?

Pam rubbed Lightning's coat with a clear cloth until it shined. It was so good to know Lightning was healthy again. But she would only stay healthy if Pam could find that girl and tell her to stop feeding Lightning apples.

Pam could see that the riding lesson was still going on in the rink. She wondered why Lulu and Anna had stopped and were cantering their ponies toward her.

Anna reached Pam first. After she halted, she leaned over in the saddle. "I remember

where I saw that fancy racing bike."

"You know the mystery girl?" Pam said.

"No," Anna answered. "But I know where to find her."

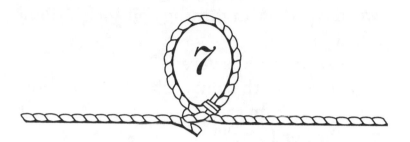

Stop!

A few minutes later, the Pony Pals were on Pony Pal Trail. They started talking about how to catch the girl.

"I've only seen the bike a couple of times," Anna said. "And that was early in the morning."

"How early?" Pam asked.

"Around seven. I saw her from my bedroom window. I noticed because it was so early and the bike went by so fast, like in a race."

"Were the two days you saw her the two days that Lightning got sick?" Pam asked.

"Yes," Anna answered.

"Those are the days she came by our place, too," Pam said. "So why don't we just wait for her there?"

"I don't think she'll go on Riddle Road again," Lulu said. "Not after we all yelled at her and everything."

"She's probably afraid of Woolie," Anna added. "People on bikes don't like dogs coming after them."

"We should wait for her on Main Street tomorrow morning," Lulu said.

With Anna leading the way, they turned off Pony Pal Trail onto a trail that led to the Wiggins Estate. Acorn whinnied happily. All the ponies put more energy into their walk. They loved to go into the Wiggins Estate with its great woodland trails and big fields.

"You should come to my house early tomorrow morning," Anna said. "We'll wait for the girl on Main Street."

"How are we going to get her to stop?" Lulu asked.

"She really speeds on that bike," Pam said.

"I've got an idea," Anna said. "Let's make a big sign. We'll stand by the side of the road and hold it up."

"Great," Pam said.

"It should be just a few words so it's easy to read," Lulu said.

"What's it going to say?" Anna asked.

"Something to trick her into stopping," Lulu suggested. "How about, YOU WON A BIG PRIZE!?"

"She'd never believe that," Pam said.

They'd reached the edge of two big open fields divided by a low stone wall. This was one of the Pony Pals' favorite spots for galloping and jumping. "Let's work our ponies here for a while," Lulu suggested.

Anna and Lulu galloped and jumped

their ponies around the field three times. But Pam jumped only once because Lightning had just been sick. While she and Lightning watched the others, Pam tried to think of what the sign should say. YOU HURT MY PONY! was her first idea. But she knew that wasn't very good. Neither was, I'LL HAVE YOU ARRESTED IF YOU DON'T STOP FEEDING MY PONY. She hoped that Lulu and Anna would have some better ideas.

The Pony Pals stopped to rest and let the ponies drink from Badd Brook. Sitting on the rocks by the water, they talked about their ideas for what the sign should say.

Lulu and Anna agreed that Pam's ideas sounded too angry.

Anna wanted to draw a picture of a dead pony surrounded by apples. Pam and Lulu thought that would be too hard for a girl riding by on a bike to see.

But Lulu had another idea that they all agreed was perfect.

"I can make the sign tonight," Anna said. "I've got lots of art supplies."

"When we get home I'll write the words down for you," Lulu offered. "So you don't make any spelling mistakes."

The next morning Pam woke with a real alarm clock instead of her Woolie bark-alarm. She was getting up an hour earlier than usual. By five-thirty she was out in the paddock, keeping an eye on Riddle Road, just in case the girl did come by and try to feed Lightning again. She didn't.

Then Pam fed Lightning and did her morning chores. By six-fifteen she was riding onto Pony Pal Trail in the early morning mist.

Cantering on the dirt path between the tall trees, Pam thought about what life was like in the time of Black Beauty. There were no trucks, tractors, or cars. Horses, not machines, plowed fields. I wish I had lived in those times, Pam thought. I bet back then people weren't wasting their time in dumb horse shows, competing for a bunch of stupid ribbons. They needed horses for important things.

By six-thirty Pam rode up to the Harley paddock. Anna and Lulu were waiting for her. They helped her unsaddle Lightning and put her in the paddock with Acorn and Snow White. Then the Pony Pals went to Main Street and stood at the edge of the town green with their sign.

"What if she sees us and goes the other way?" Lulu asked.

"Or whizzes right past us," Anna added. "We could never catch her."

"We'd better smile and look friendly," Lulu suggested. "That way she'll know we're nice."

"I can't smile," Pam said. "I'm too mad at her."

"Do it for Lightning," Anna suggested.

"Okay," Pam agreed.

Just then they saw the girl speeding up

Main Street on her racing bike.

The Pony Pals put on their brightest smiles and held up the sign. It read:

STOP. MUST TALK TO YOU.
VERY IMPORTANT.

The biker was so focused on pedaling fast, she didn't notice them or the sign.

Pam yelled out, "Hey! Look!"

The girl turned her head in their direction and screeched her bike to a stop. Pam saw that the girl was looking at a stopwatch. The Pony Pals ran over to her. She was out of breath when she spoke. "I was having my best time ever," she said. "This had better be important."

"It is," Pam said.

"You're the kid who scared me yesterday," the girl said to Pam. She read the sign that was now on the ground. "What's all this?" she asked. "Is this some silly game?"

"It's not a game," Pam said angrily. "You almost killed my pony."

"Don't be ridiculous," the girl said.

"It's true," Anna said. "You gave Lightning apples."

"Horses love apples," the girl said. "Give me a break."

"It was too much food with all the other stuff she eats," Lulu said. "Lightning got really sick."

"And she almost died," Pam added.

The girl was looking at them as if they were crazy. "Why should I believe you?" she asked. "You're some bored kids who don't have enough to do on vacation. And you've ruined my practice session."

Pam felt tears forming in her eyes, but she was determined not to cry. If she cried the girl would really think they were babies and *never* believe them. Then she might continue overfeeding horses. Maybe even Lightning.

"Look, we're not going to get you into trouble or anything," Pam said. "But you've got to understand. If horses eat too much they get very, very sick. They can't throw up."

"Can't throw up?" the girl laughed. "Now I really know you're fooling around. I'm out of here." She got on her bike to ride off. "And don't ever bother me again."

The Gift

The Pony Pals knew that they couldn't let the girl get away. Anna grabbed the front wheel of the girl's bike and Lulu grabbed the back wheel.

"Let go of my bike," the girl said.

Anna and Lulu held on tight.

"Right now!" the girl shouted. "You'll throw off the alignment."

Anna and Lulu didn't let go.

"Little kids can be such a pain!" the girl exclaimed.

"We'll let go, if you promise not to ride away," Anna said.

"Okay, I promise," the girl said.

Pam pointed to a bench on the town green. "Let's go over there."

"Only for a minute," the girl said.

Pam and the girl sat on the bench. Anna and Lulu leaned on the fence facing them.

"You know all about bikes, right?" Pam asked.

"Sure I do," the girl answered. "I'm a state champion in distance racing. There's a big Eastern Division race next week and you've just ruined my practice run — and the alignment on my bike."

"You know all about bikes," Pam said. "Well, we know all about ponies."

"Pam's father's a veterinarian," Lulu added.

"And we all know that if horses overeat, it can make them very sick," Pam continued.

"Because they can't throw up?" the girl asked with a laugh.

Anna spoke in her most serious voice, "It may sound funny to you that horses don't throw up. But, for horses, it's not funny at all."

The girl looked around at the Pony Pals. She turned serious herself. "You guys are telling the truth, aren't you?" she said. "About the throwing-up stuff and about the pony being sick."

They all nodded solemnly.

The girl took off her helmet. She had the reddest hair that Pam had ever seen. "By the way," the girl said, "I'm Diane McGann."

The Pony Pals introduced themselves, too.

Diane wasn't mad at them anymore for interrupting her ride. She seemed a little frightened when she asked, "Did I really make that beautiful pony sick?"

The three girls nodded again.

"How many times did you feed her?" Pam asked.

"Twice before the time you stopped me,"

Diane answered. "Your pony's so beautiful that I started bringing her apples. That way she'd come and stay with me awhile. I really made her sick?"

"It wasn't your fault," Anna said. "It's not like the wicked queen in Snow White. You didn't know any better. And the apples weren't poisoned. We checked."

"I'd never hurt an animal on purpose," Diane said. "Even a dog that's barking at me when I'm riding on my bike. I never kick at them like some people do." Pam could see that Diane was upset. "Was your pony *very* sick?" she asked.

"*Very*," Pam said. "If it had happened again Lightning could have died."

Diane was silent for a few seconds. Then she asked, "How does she feel now?"

"My dad said she'll probably be okay as long as she doesn't overeat again. I can't ride her too much for a couple of days."

"She's not a hundred percent better then," Diane said.

"Promise me you'll never ever feed her again," Pam said.

"Of course I won't," Diane answered. "I'm just worried she won't get all better."

The town clock struck the half hour. "It's seven-thirty," Diane said. She got up and put her helmet back on. "I've got to get to the gym for my workout," she said. "My coach is waiting for me. He'll think I had an accident or something."

She got on her bike. "Don't worry," she told Pam, "I'll never feed her again." She rode off the green and up Main Street.

When she was out of sight, the Pony Pals jumped up, hit high fives, and shouted, "All *right!*" Then they went to Off-Main Diner to celebrate.

The Pony Pals were glad to see that their favorite booth in the back was empty.

"Mom said we don't have to pay for breakfast," Anna said, "because of vacation and everything. But we have to take our own orders."

Pam took a pad and pencil off the counter and took the orders.

Anna ordered blueberry pancakes. Lulu wanted Granola with banana and strawberries. Pam wrote down, "scrambled eggs with ham and homefries," for herself.

While the Pony Pals were eating, they congratulated themselves again about how they got Diane McGann to stop and listen to them. They all agreed that she was totally innocent of any crime against Lightning.

"She's really sorry about what she did," Pam said. "I could tell."

Anna waved toward the door of the diner. "Look," she told Lulu and Pam. "Ms. Wiggins just came in."

When Ms. Wiggins saw the Pony Pals, she came right over to their booth. They all liked Ms. Wiggins, especially Anna. And Ms. Wiggins loved horses as much as they did. She still had her Shetland pony she rode as a young girl. The Pony Pals usually didn't visit Ms. Wiggins when they rode on her trails on Wiggins Estate. They knew that she liked to be alone to do her paintings. But sometimes Ms. Wiggins left her big house and property to eat at the diner. Like everyone in town, she loved the food at Off-Main Diner.

"Well, well," Ms. Wiggins said, "I'm so glad to see you all here." She held out three packages wrapped in colorfully decorated brown paper. "Anna, I thought I'd have your mother give you these. Now I can do it myself." She handed each of the girls a gift.

"You open yours first, Anna," Lulu said.

Anna carefully opened the gift so the hand-painted paper wouldn't tear. She held up a periwinkle-blue satin vest. "Oh-hh, it's beautiful," Anna exclaimed.

"I made it plenty big," Ms. Wiggins said, "so you can wear it over a jacket. It's for the horse show."

Lulu opened her package. She got a vest,

too. "I love it," she said as she slipped the vest on. "Thank you so much."

Pam unwrapped her gift, but she didn't unfold the vest.

Mrs. Harley and the waiter, Fred, came over to the booth. Everyone in the diner was stretching their necks to get a look at the vests.

"Mom, you told her our color, didn't you?" Anna said.

Mrs. Harley smiled and nodded.

"Then I remembered this fabric," Ms. Wiggins told them. "It's been hanging around my place for years. I guess it was just waiting to become vests for the Pony Pals."

"They're perfect," Lulu said. "Thank you."

Anna jumped up and gave Ms. Wiggins a hug. "Thank you," she said. "Thank you."

"Are you coming to the show?" Lulu asked Ms. Wiggins.

"Absolutely," she answered. "Winston

and I are giving the younger children cart rides. My old pony loves to be in horse shows and I do, too. I'm particularly looking forward to seeing you three girls there."

"Thank you for the vest, it's very pretty," Pam said to Ms. Wiggins. "But I'm not going to be in the horse show."

The Chicken-Pox Horse Show

The day before the horse show, the Pony Pals met at the Harley paddock.

"Where are we going to trail ride today?" Pam asked.

"Let's ride over to Olson's farm," Anna suggested. "I want to see how long it will take to get there from my house."

"Great idea," Lulu said. "Snow White can see the ring. That way the farm won't be strange for her tomorrow."

Pam agreed to the plan. "I like the trail to Olson's," she said.

"Did you tell your parents how we solved the mystery of the apple feeder?" Anna asked Pam.

"Yes," Pam answered. "They think we'd all make great detectives."

The Pony Pals rode along Main Street. Then they made a right onto Belgo Road. Suddenly Snow White threw her head back. "Whoa, girl," Lulu said. As Lulu calmed down her pony, Pam and Anna looked around to see what had spooked Snow White.

They saw Diane McGann riding her bike up from behind them.

"Hi," Diane said as she rode alongside them.

They all said hi back to her.

"Don't ride your bike close to horses," Pam said. "It could scare them."

"Sorry," Diane said as she got off her bike. "How's Lightning doing?" she asked Pam. "She looks okay."

"She's all right now," Pam said.

"I've been so worried about her," Diane said. "It's all I've been thinking about."

They'd passed Off-Main Diner and reached the turnoff for the trail. When the Pony Pals halted their ponies, Diane stopped, too.

"Where are you all going now?" she asked.

"Over to Olson's farm," Anna answered.

"We're in a horse show there tomorrow," Lulu explained.

"Good for you," Diane said. "I'm going to be in a big bike race myself next weekend. In Virginia."

Through tension in the reins, Pam could feel that Lightning wanted to go over to Diane. Lightning wants to see if she has any of those apples on her, Pam thought. She held back her pony.

"I've never seen anyone ride a bike as fast as you do," Anna said.

Diane wasn't paying attention to what Anna was saying. She was looking at

271

Lightning. "Can I pat her on the neck?" she asked Pam.

"Sure," Pam said. "That won't hurt her."

Diane walked up to Lightning and rubbed the smooth reddish-brown length of Lightning's neck.

"I'm going to go to that horse show," Diane said, "so I can see for sure that Lightning is okay."

"Don't you have to practice bike racing?" Pam asked.

"I can take a few hours off," Diane said. She scratched the white upside-down heart on Lightning's forehead. "I don't think I'm going to win in Virginia anyway," she said. "I haven't been riding very well this week."

"Lightning's not going to be in the horse show," Pam said.

Diane looked up at Pam with alarm. "I thought she was all better."

"We just don't like to be in horse shows," Pam answered.

A red motor scooter whizzed down Main Street. "Uh-oh," Diane said. "That was my coach. I'm on the wrong road and I shouldn't have stopped. Now I've got to try to catch up to him."

She got on her bike and sped off.

"She still doesn't believe that Lightning's okay," Anna said.

"I know," Pam said.

The Olson farm was a busy place that day. People were setting up jumps and decorating them with potted flowers. Volunteer firemen were unloading a big barbecue pit from the back of a pickup truck. And Pam's mother and Mr. Olson were giving directions for putting up the judges' stands. Another woman was installing a loudspeaker system for the ringmasters.

"I can't wait for tomorrow," Anna said. "I think Acorn's going to do really well."

"You and Acorn looked great in practice," Lulu told her.

"You and Snow White did, too," Anna said.

Pam felt unhappy. She was remembering that the only horse show she'd been in was held right here, at Olson's farm. She wanted to get away as fast as she could.

"Let's go," she told her friends.

"Okay," Lulu said.

"We can go back to my place," Anna said, "and make the rest of our decorations for tomorrow. Will you help us, Pam?"

"Sure," Pam said. "Why not?"

Even though it was her turn to lead on the trail, Pam was feeling depressed and wanted to be last. She told Lulu to take her place.

Later, in Anna's bedroom, the girls wrapped blue and silver ribbon around Anna's and Lulu's riding crops. Then they stuck periwinkle-blue stars on the outside edge of their saddle blankets and on the bands of their helmets.

"Pam, this would be so much more fun if you were going to be in the show, too," Lulu said.

"I told you I hate horse shows," Pam told her. "I always have. Ever since I was little."

"She was only in one," Anna told Lulu. "The chicken-pox horse show."

"The chicken-pox horse show?" Lulu said. "What's that?"

"What are you talking about, Anna?" Pam asked.

"Don't you remember?" Anna said. "You came down with chicken pox during that horse show. You were the first one to get sick. Then I and just about everybody else in our riding class got chicken pox."

The Pony Pals were silent for a second. They were all remembering what it was like to have chicken pox.

"That's it," Lulu said.

"What?" Pam asked.

"Why you don't like to be in horse shows."

"Because of chicken pox?" Pam said. "That's not why. You don't understand. No one understands." She got up. "I'm going home."

Don't Stop!

"Pam, please stay," Lulu said.

Pam sat back down on the edge of Anna's bed.

"When I got chicken pox I felt awful," Lulu told her. "It was when Dad and I first moved to England. I kept telling him that I was miserable and that I hated England. It turned out I really loved England. What I hated was having chicken pox."

"I couldn't even *sit* on a horse when I had it," Anna said. "Pam, you got all those spots during a horse show."

"Don't you see?" Lulu added. "Chicken pox ruined the show for you."

Listening to her friends talk, Pam remembered the horse show better than ever before. Not just the part about not getting any ribbons. Now she remembered the part about chicken pox. After the show, when she took off her blouse, she saw that her belly was covered in itchy red spots. She also had a fever and felt very nervous. Just the way she felt during the horse show.

"How can you know what it feels like to be in a horse show if you had chicken pox during the only one you were ever in?" Lulu asked.

"I never thought about it that way," Pam answered.

"You hated chicken pox," Lulu and Anna said in unison.

"How can anybody compete when they're sick?" Lulu said.

"Please say you'll be in the show tomorrow," Anna pleaded.

"Your mother says you and Lightning

would do great in competition," Lulu said.

"She's your teacher," Anna added. "So she should know."

"I don't care what my mother thinks," Pam snapped. "I'm sick of everybody nagging me about horse shows and about being the teacher's daughter."

Anna put her arm around Pam's shoulder. "I just think you should give it another try," she said.

"You could enter the Pleasure Division where you do all the things we do when we trail ride," Lulu suggested.

"Like opening and closing gates," Anna added. "And jumping over logs. Just pretend you're on a trail ride and you won't be nervous," Lulu said.

"Okay," Pam finally agreed. "I'll be in the horse show."

Anna and Lulu raised their hands to do a high five. But Pam stopped them. "Wait a minute," she said. "Okay . . . I'll be in the horse show *if* you help me do something first."

When Anna and Lulu heard what Pam wanted them to do, they happily agreed. Then the Pony Pals all raised their hands, shouted "All *right!*" and hit their high fives.

The next morning, Pam woke up before her Woolie bark-alarm again. It was still dark outside while she dressed and ate a bowl of cereal. But by the time she'd fed Lightning and saddled her, the sun was coming up.

"We're going to be in a horse show today," she told her pony. "I was sick during the last horse show I was in. But today I'm healthy. And so are you."

Lightning nickered and nudged Pam's shoulder.

Lulu and Anna were waiting for Pam at the other end of Pony Pal Trail. Anna held three cardboard signs. Each one was sta-

pled to a stick. Pam unsaddled Lightning and let her into the paddock with Snow White and Acorn. Then Anna passed out the signs.

"Okay," Pam said. "Let's go."

The three girls went on to Main Street and waited. And waited.

"What if she doesn't come this way today?" Lulu asked.

"She'll come," Pam said. "She's probably just riding slower today."

A minute later the Pony Pals saw Diane McGann pumping her bike up Main Street.

"She's not taking the hill very fast," Anna said.

"Maybe she's feeling awful that she made my pony sick and is worried that Lightning's not better," Pam said. She thought about how lonely it must be for Diane to ride her bike all by herself for hours at a time. And she thought about how lucky she was to have great pony-riding friends.

When Diane got to the top of the hill, she

looked up and saw the Pony Pals. They held up their cardboard signs.

Anna's sign read:

DON'T STOP!

Lulu's sign read:

KEEP RIDING!

And Pam's sign read:

LIGHTNING IN HORSE SHOW!

Diane read the signs as she slowly rode by the girls. Her face lit up with a big smile.

"Come on, Diane!" Anna shouted. "You can do it."

Diane looked at the road ahead of her.

"You're a winner, Diane!" Lulu called out. "Go for it."

Diane started pedaling harder.

"Do it for Lightning!" Pam shouted.

Diane didn't even turn around. She was totally concentrating on biking as she sped out of sight.

The Parade

The Pony Pals went back to the Harley paddock to give their ponies a final grooming for the horse show. Lulu's grandmother, who was a hairdresser, walked across the paddock toward them.

"It's a special day," she told them. "I thought you could use my professional services."

The girls were all surprised because they knew that Grandmother Sanders didn't like horses very much. But she was very cheerful as she taught the Pony Pals how to braid periwinkle-blue yarn into their ponies' manes.

After Grandmother Sanders left, the girls painted the ponies' hooves with oil. And Pam washed Lightning's upside-down heart so it would shine. She thought about the first time she saw that white marking, and how much she loved her pony. "I can't wait to show everyone at the horse show what a wonderful pony Lightning is," she told her friends.

The Pony Pals mounted their ponies for the ride over to Olson's. "Look," Anna said, "the sky is the same shade of blue as our vests and decorations."

Pam looked at the periwinkle-blue sky, and smiled. The Pony Pals were on their way to the horse show and she felt great.

"You know," she said to her friends, "I feel a lot different than I did the first time I was going to a horse show. This is *fun*."

Anna and Lulu smiled at one another, but they *didn't* say, "I told you so."

*　　*　　*

Olson's farm was bustling with people and horses. Everywhere she looked, Pam saw horses. There were horses being led out of trailers, horses being ridden across the field, horses on leads. The Pony Pals dismounted and led their ponies over to the registration table.

After they had registered, they looked at the schedule of classes in their programs.

"My Pony Hunter classes are in Ring Two," Lulu said. "Anna's Short Stirrup classes are in Ring One."

Pam saw that her class, Open Pleasure Pony, was also in Ring One. "It looks like we'll be running back and forth between the rings if we want to see one another," she said.

"And sometimes we'll be competing at the same time," Lulu added.

"Ten minutes until the first class," Mr. Olson announced.

Pam was feeling a little nervous. But not

the kind of nervous that made her unhappy. It was the kind of nervous that made her feel excited.

First she watched Anna and Acorn win a second-place ribbon for Short Stirrup Equitation over fences. Then she watched Lulu in Ring Two in Pony Hunter over fences. Lulu and Snow White won a first-place blue ribbon.

"Rema will be so happy," Lulu told Pam.

When it was time for Open Pleasure Pony, Pam told Lightning, "It's just like being on a trail ride. We'll do just fine."

And so they did.

Mrs. Crandal came up to Pam as she was exiting the ring with a red ribbon on Lightning's bridle. Pam figured her mother would say how proud she was of her and that she knew all along that she would do well in horse shows. But she didn't. Instead, her mother said, "You know, Pam, I'm very happy you're in the horse show. Not because I expect you to win ribbons. But because I think horse shows are a fun part of being a rider. Are you having a good time?"

"Yes," Pam admitted. She leaned over and patted Lightning on the neck. "Lightning is, too."

Mrs. Crandal scratched Lightning's head. "Congratulations to both of you," she said.

"Thanks, Mom," Pam said. Pam was glad that her mother understood. Then her mother went off to Ring Two to help her students.

As she dismounted, Pam saw Diane McGann walking toward her. "I didn't even know you were here," Pam told Diane.

"I got here just in time to see you," Diane told her. "Lightning looks so beautiful with all the blue decorations. And the way you jumped over the stone wall! It was all terrific. Congratulations."

"Do you see how healthy Lightning is?" Pam asked.

Diane smiled. "I finally believe she's

okay," she said. "I felt just awful before."

"I know," Pam said. "How was your bike ride this morning?"

"Better," she answered. "I picked up some speed after you guys cheered me on." She looked around at all the horse show activity. "Being here reminds me of how much fun bike races can be," she said. "That's when I get to be with other racers. We have lots of fun, too."

"Pony Hunter Under Saddle in Ring Two," the loudspeaker announced.

"Do you want to watch Lulu and Snow White jump?" Pam asked Diane.

Diane stroked Lightning's cheek. "I can't," she said. "I need to clock another thirty miles on my bike this afternoon."

Pam said, "Oh, that's too bad."

"No it's not," Diane said. "I have a race to win next week and I want to be ready. You all inspired me. Good luck with the rest of the show."

"Thanks," said Pam. "Bye."

Pam led Lightning over to Ring Two so

they could watch Lulu in her next class.

The afternoon at the horse show was as much fun as the morning. Pam made sure that Jack and Jill got cart rides with Ms. Wiggins and Winston. "I'm so glad you decided to be in the show." Ms. Wiggins told Pam.

"Me, too," Pam said. "Thanks again for the vest."

"I haven't seen the three of you together once today," Ms. Wiggins said. "But I expect before the day is over, I'll see you riding side by side."

"When?" Pam asked.

"You'll see," Ms. Wiggins answered with a wink.

After the last ribbons and the championship cups were awarded, Mr. Olson announced: "The ponies and horses in this competition are so beautifully turned out that we're going to have a parade." A lot of people cheered.

"You have ten minutes to line up behind the pony cart in Ring One," Mr. Olson continued. "Once around the ring and then over to Ring Two."

Pam saw that Ms. Wiggins was inviting the twins, Jack and Jill, to ride with her at the head of the parade. They were jumping up and down with excitement.

"And behind the pony cart," Mr. Olson was saying, "I'd like to see Pam Crandal, Anna Harley, and Lulu Sanders."

Pam straightened out the ribbons that decorated Lightning's bridle. Then she mounted and rode up alongside Anna and Lulu. Other riders and their horses lined up behind them.

Pam imagined how she would have felt if she hadn't been in the horse show. Lightning and I would have missed so much fun, she thought. And there would have been only two girls with periwinkle-blue colors.

"All right, let's go," Mr. Olson announced.

Suddenly, lively marching music filled the air. Lightning, Snow White, and Acorn

held their heads high and stepped out into a brisk walk. Pam loved how the three ponies were keeping in step with one another as they paraded around the ring.

Before the Pony Pals dismounted at the end of the parade, a woman with a camera came up to them. "I'm a reporter for the *County Times*," she said. "I'd love to get a picture."

The three girls sat proudly in their saddles and smiled at the camera. The reporter clicked off a few shots. Then she took out her notebook and pencil. "I need to know who you girls are, for the caption under the picture," she said.

Pam, Anna, and Lulu answered together. "We're the Pony Pals," they said.

Give Me Back My Pony

For my nephew, Chase

The author thanks her riding teachers, Linda Bushnell of Fair Weather Farm and Jeannette van Mill of Moles Hill Farm.

Thanks also to Elvia Gignoux and Helen Perelman for editorial assistance.

The Last Trail Ride

Lulu Sanders snapped her saddlebag closed and hurried out the back door. It was the first day of summer vacation and the Pony Pals were meeting on Pony Pal Trail for a whole day with their ponies.

By the time Lulu climbed the paddock fence, her pony, Snow White, was there to greet her. "I love you, Snow White," Lulu said, giving the white pony a hug.

Anna Harley, who lived next door, was climbing over the fence, too. But her pony didn't run up to her. Instead, Acorn scooted in the opposite direction. He was the most playful of the Pony Pal ponies and loved playing hard-to-get with Anna.

Lulu helped Anna catch Acorn. Then the girls groomed and saddled up their ponies. Finally, they rode onto the mile-and-a-half trail that connected their paddock with Pam Crandal's paddock.

Pam and Lightning met them halfway up Pony Pal Trail. "It's hot enough to take the ponies into the lake," Pam said.

"Great!" said Anna. "It'll be the first time this summer. I just know they'll love being in the water." The girls directed their ponies onto the Wiggins estate. The trails there led to Lake Appamapog.

When they reached the lakefront, Snow White pawed playfully at the wet sand. Lulu directed Snow White with her seat and her legs to go forward into the water. Snow White neighed as she walked into the cool lake. Anna followed on Acorn. Lightning was more timid than the other ponies about going into the lake. But when she saw Acorn and Snow White happily prancing around in the shallow water, she went in, too. The girls laughed and hooted as the water splashed up around their ponies' legs.

After playing in the lake, the ponies took naps under the trees while the Pony Pals ate their lunch. The girls agreed that the lake was a great new place to have fun with their ponies.

"Let's take them here again tomorrow," Pam said.

"I heard on the radio that tomorrow's going to be even hotter than today," Lulu said.

"We'll do it all sum — " Anna stopped in the middle of the word. The Pony Pals exchanged sad glances. They were remembering that soon Lulu wouldn't have a pony. Any day now, Snow White's *real* owner, Rema Baxter, would be coming home from boarding school. Then Lulu would have to give Snow White back. They also remembered that Lulu was going to move away very soon.

"I just can't believe you won't be here anymore, Lulu," Anna said. "Nothing will be the same without you."

"Lulu, do you know where you and your dad are going to live yet?" Pam asked.

"Not yet," Lulu answered. "It'll probably be someplace far away though. Like Africa. He mostly likes to write about large animals, like elephants."

Lulu had been living with her grandmother while her father worked on a wildlife research project in the Amazon jungle in Brazil. Lulu's mother died when Lulu was four years old. She wasn't so sad about not having a mother because she was very close to her father. She was glad that she and her dad would be together again soon. But that would mean leaving Wiggins and her Pony Pals.

"Wherever you go," Pam said, "I sure hope they have ponies."

"No pony can ever take the place of Snow White," Lulu said.

After lunch the girls put the bridles back on their ponies, mounted, and rode back to the trail. "Come on, don't be sad," Lulu said to her friends. "Let's have as much fun as we can while I'm still here." Then she moved Snow White into a canter.

Anna and Acorn started to canter, too. "Let's trail ride every day," Anna shouted.

Pam and Lightning cantered up beside Anna and Acorn. "And have barn sleepovers," Pam added.

When the Pony Pals came off Pony Pal Trail at Pam's house, Lulu saw the five-year-old Crandal twins, Jack and Jill, running toward them.

"Lulu, your grandma called. Rema's father called her to ask where was Snow White," shouted Jill.

"You gotta bring Snow White back right now," shouted Jack.

Mrs. Crandal came up beside Lulu and Snow White and explained everything very clearly. Rema Baxter was coming home from boarding school the next day. The Baxters had already put in a new paddock fence and ordered feed and straw. They wanted Snow White settled in her own field and stable, for Rema.

"Mr. Baxter seemed annoyed that he couldn't reach you all day," Mrs. Crandal added. "So you'd better take Snow White right over."

Lulu pressed her cheek against Snow White's warm, smooth neck as she listened to Mrs. Crandal. She thought about the wonderful time she and Snow White had that morning playing in the lake and trail riding. Today was their last trail ride and she hadn't even known it.

Getting Ready for Rema

"Oh, Lulu, I wish you didn't have to give Snow White back," Anna said.

"We'll go to the Baxters' with you," Pam told her.

The Pony Pals got on their ponies and rode them down Riddle Road toward the Baxters' property.

Turning left onto Lilac Lane, Lulu remembered when she saw the beautiful white pony caught in an old barbed wire. Everyone said that Lulu had saved Snow White's life. But she couldn't have done it without Pam and Anna. That was how they all had met — rescuing Snow White. Lulu always thought of that day as the beginning of the Pony Pals.

Lulu would miss her friends terribly when she left Wiggins. Anna Harley lived right next door to Lulu's grandmother. Their ponies shared the paddock behind the Harleys' house. Lulu thought Anna was a great friend. She was funny and full of energy. She was also a terrific artist.

Lulu trotted Snow White up beside Anna and Acorn. "When we're pen pals," she told Anna, "don't worry about spelling mistakes, okay? Just be sure to write. And draw me pictures, too." Anna promised she would.

Lulu knew there wouldn't be any spelling errors in Pam's letters. Pam Crandal got A's in all her subjects at school. But Lulu was afraid that Pam would be too busy to write her letters. The Crandals ran an animal clinic on their property. Dr. Crandal was a veterinarian, and Mrs. Crandal taught horseback riding. There were always a lot of animals at the Crandals', which meant a lot of chores for Pam.

Pam, bringing up the rear, called out, "Don't worry, Lulu. I'll find time to write you. I'll write every week." Lulu sometimes thought that the Pony Pals could read one another's minds.

When they reached the Baxters' property, the three girls dismounted. The new fence looked safe for ponies. But the girls made sure that there weren't any pieces of barbed wired left in the field. They knew how dangerous barbed wire could be from having seen what it did to Snow White. After they let their ponies into the paddock, they went to the stable to make sure it was ready for Snow White, too.

"This stable is filthy!" Pam shouted when they walked through the stable door.

Lulu could see that Pam was right. There were piles of dirty straw, dust, and cobwebs everywhere. The supplies had been delivered, but no one had put them away. "I can't

leave Snow White in this mess," Lulu said. "What if she gets into that food and over-eats? What if she wants to lie down in her stall?"

"Let's get to work," Pam said.

Anna started sweeping, Pam unloaded feed into the bins, and Lulu cleaned out the water buckets. Lulu felt a little nudge on her back. She turned around to see that Snow White had come up to her. The pony looked at Lulu as if to say, "What's going on? When are we going home?"

"This is your real home," Lulu told Snow White. "I was just taking care of you while Rema was away at school. You'll remember her when you see her tomorrow."

Snow White snorted and went back to Acorn and Lightning.

"I don't think Snow White even recognizes this place," Lulu told Anna and Pam.

"She only lived here a few weeks before you got her," said Pam. "The Baxters are new to Wiggins."

"That means Rema won't know any kids when she's home this summer," Lulu said. "Maybe she could go trail riding with you guys."

"Rema! A Pony Pal?" Anna exclaimed. "Never! I can't stand her. She's so snobby."

Pam and Lulu couldn't help laughing. "You've never even met her, Anna," Pam pointed out.

Lulu put a hand on Anna's shoulder. "You've got to give Rema a chance," she said. "For Snow White's sake. Snow White's going to really miss Acorn and Lightning."

"Well, I'll let Rema ride with us only because of Snow White," Anna said. "But she'll never be a Pony Pal."

"She's too old anyway," Pam said to Anna. "She's around fourteen. Like your sister. Maybe we should introduce them."

"If *I* don't like Rema," Anna responded, "my sister won't either."

Lulu hoped with all her heart that Anna

was wrong about Rema Baxter. She wanted Rema to be the nicest person in the world. For Snow White's sake.

The three girls made a final inspection of the stable.

"Couldn't be cleaner," Pam said.

"We've done everything," said Anna.

"There's one thing I haven't done," Lulu told the others.

"What?" Anna and Pam asked in unison.

"I haven't said good-bye to Snow White."

"You want us to wait for you?" Pam asked.

"I think I want to be alone with Snow White," Lulu said.

As Pam and Anna rode off on their ponies, Snow White neighed and ran along the fence. She seemed to be saying, "Where are you going without me? Hey, wait up."

Lulu played with Snow White for a while. First they chased one another around the paddock. Then they stood under the shade of a tree and Lulu sang Snow White some of the pony's favorite songs, like "Jingle Bells." Finally, Lulu gave Snow White a bucket of water and a handful of oats. She wrote a note and posted it on the stable door.

Dear Mr. and Mrs. Baxter:
   Snow White has eaten her dinner.

        Sincerely,
        Lucinda (Lulu) Sanders

P.S.
Tell Rema I said "Welcome, home."
P.P.S.
Snow White is the most wonderful pony in the world.

Lulu rubbed Snow White's smooth white neck and told the pony, "Rema will be home tomorrow." She gave Snow White a hug and a kiss. Snow White sighed. "I'll never forget you, Snow White," Lulu said.

Lulu didn't want Snow White to see her cry. So she didn't look back when she climbed over the fence and ran down Lilac Lane. She was still running — and sobbing — when she turned the corner onto Mudge Road.

"Lulu! Wait!" Lulu looked up to see Pam and Anna walking toward her — without their ponies.

"We came to walk you home," Anna said.

The three friends held hands as they walked toward Main Street. No one spoke. Lulu knew that Pam and Anna felt sad about Snow White. They were her best friends. Soon she would be saying good-bye to them, too.

"I hate saying good-bye," Lulu said sadly.

"Me too," Pam said.

"Me three," Anna said.

The Runaway Pony

When Lulu arrived home, she was still feeling sad. But her grandmother greeted her with some news that cheered her up. They had gotten a telegram from Lulu's father.

> Leaving Jungle.
> In U.S.A. Tuesday.
> Love. Dad.

Lulu was so happy and excited about seeing her dad, she had a hard time falling asleep that night. But she must have, because the next thing she knew a voice was saying, "Lucinda, wake up."

Lulu opened her eyes to see her grandmother leaning over her. She had a strange smile on her face.

Lulu sat up. "Is he here?" she asked excitedly. "Is Dad here?"

"Not yet," her grandmother said. "It's only Sunday. But someone else is here."

"Who?" Lulu asked.

"That pony of yours," Grandmother answered.

"Snow White?!" Lulu shouted. "But I gave her back to Rema."

Lulu jumped out of bed and ran to the window. Grandmother was right. Snow White was in the paddock nibbling dewy grass next to Acorn. Just like always.

Lulu ran down the stairs and outside.

Anna was running across the yard, too. "I just saw Snow White out the kitchen window," she said to Lulu excitedly. "I was going to get you."

The two girls went into the paddock. Snow White neighed and ran over to them. "Snow White," Lulu said, "you ran away."

"She didn't run away," Anna said. "To her *this* is home. She ran home to Acorn and to you." Anna stroked the pony's neck. "What a smart pony."

"I better go back in and call the Baxters," Lulu said.

But the Baxters weren't home. Mr. Baxter's voice on the answering machine asked callers to leave a message. Lulu told the machine, "Snow White came back to the paddock she lived in when I was taking care of her. She didn't get hurt or anything. I'm bringing her back to you. Oh . . . this is Lulu Sanders. Thank you. Bye."

By the time Lulu had breakfast and went back outside, Pam and Lightning were also in the paddock.

"I bet the Baxters didn't even notice that Snow White was missing," Pam said. "They shouldn't have a pony."

"It's not their pony," Lulu said. "It's Rema's. Let's bring Snow White back."

"I bet she'll just run away again," Anna said.

"That'd be awful," Pam said. "It's dangerous for a pony to be loose on the roads. She could get hit by a truck or something."

"I know," Lulu said. "But she won't run away when Rema's there."

Lulu thought about Rema and Snow White. She hadn't pictured them together before. There would be another girl giving Snow White good morning hugs. Another girl riding her and cantering like the wind. Another girl singing Snow White songs and grooming her.

"We better go," Lulu told her friends.

Lulu borrowed a bridle from Anna. Then, because she didn't have a saddle anymore, Lulu mounted Snow White bareback. "Let's take Pony Pal Trail instead of Main Street," she said. "It'll be safer."

The Pony Pals never thought they would

trail ride together again, and here they were on Pony Pal Trail.

"I missed us all riding together like this," Anna said.

"We just did it yesterday," Pam said.

"I know," said Anna. "But I miss it already."

When they got to the Baxters' and saw that Rema wasn't home yet, Pam said, "We'll wait here with you. We can help you explain how Snow White ran away and everything."

While they all waited for Rema, Lulu groomed Snow White one more time. She wanted Snow White to look her best. She was combing out Snow White's mane when the Baxters' station wagon pulled into the driveway. The instant the car stopped, a girl jumped out of the back and ran toward the paddock. "Snow White!" she called out. "Snow White, I'm home."

Snow White pulled away from Lulu, neighed happily, and cantered toward the girl. Rema was back.

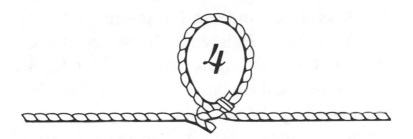

Meeting Rema

Lulu was standing in the middle of the paddock watching the happy reunion between Rema and Snow White.

Pam put her hand on Lulu's shoulder. "Come on, Lulu, let's tell Rema how Snow White ran away."

The Pony Pals walked toward Rema. "I don't like her," Anna whispered. "She's definitely a snob."

Lulu thought Rema looked nice. You could tell right away that she was older than the Pony Pals. She was taller than they were, had on a black sundress and black sandals, and used makeup.

As the Pony Pals walked toward Rema, they noticed that she was feeding Snow White a chocolate bar. "We never feed our ponies candy," Anna said.

"Well, Snow White loves chocolate," Rema said. "Who are you, anyway?"

"I'm Lulu Sanders," Lulu said. "We were waiting for you and keeping Snow White company."

"I'm Pam Crandal," Pam said. She extended her hand to shake with Rema's. Lulu wished she had thought of shaking hands, too.

"I'm Anna Harley," Anna said grumpily. Rema put out her hand to shake with Anna, but Anna pretended that she didn't see it.

"Snow White missed Lulu so much that she escaped and came back to our paddock," Anna said. "That's where she's been living with my pony, Acorn. Snow White missed Acorn, too. Our ponies are all best friends."

Rema stared at Lulu.

Lulu stared right back at her.

No one said a word.

Finally, Rema broke the silence. "So you're Lucinda Sanders," she said. "If I'd known you were so young I wouldn't have left my horse with you. You sounded older in your letters."

"Lulu knows all about *horses,*" Pam said. "And *ponies* like Snow White. She took very good care of your *pony.*"

"Is that why my *horse* ran away last night?" Rema asked.

Lulu felt awful. Why was Rema being mean to them? And why did she insist on calling Snow White a horse? Rema must know that Snow White was a pony breed and too small to be a horse. Was that what Anna would call "snobby"? It also bothered Lulu that Snow White was staying right next to Rema. She knew it was important that Snow White like her owner. But she hated that Snow White was ignoring her.

"Let's get out of here," Pam told Anna and Lulu. "I'll get Lightning."

While Pam and Anna went to get their ponies, Lulu told Rema, "We fixed up the stable for Snow White. She's been having two handfuls of oats everyday. One at —"

"I know how to take care of Snow White," Rema said. She ruffled up the hair on Snow White's forehead. "We've been together for a long time."

Snow White noticed that Lightning and Acorn were being saddled up. She walked over to Lulu and looked at her as if to say, "Okay, let's go."

"You're not going with us, Snow White," Lulu told the pony. But Snow White didn't understand. She neighed and gently nudged Lulu. To Lulu she was saying, "Come on. I want to go trail riding too."

"I'm sorry, Snow White," she whispered. "I wish you could come with us." Lulu combed out the hair on the pony's forehead that Rema had messed up.

Rema, meanwhile, was picking Snow White's white hair off her sundress. She didn't even look up when she asked Lulu,

"What do people around here do all summer? Wiggins is so boring."

"That's what I thought when I first moved here," Lulu said. "But it's really not boring at all. We go trail riding and swim in the lake. There're a lot of hiking trails. And there's a diner with really good food. Especially brownies. Sometimes we hang out there."

"I wasn't asking what *you* do," Rema said. "I meant the teenagers. Like me."

Lulu was beginning to think Anna was right about Rema Baxter. She hoped that Rema was nicer to ponies than she was to kids.

Snow White was still confused about why she wasn't being saddled up like Lightning and Acorn. The pony went over to Rema to see if she would tell her. A little string of Snow White's saliva fell on Rema's dress. "Oh, Snow White," Rema said with exasperation. "Now look what you've done!" She pushed Snow White away from her.

The Pony Pals exchanged glances. Rema

treated ponies the same way she treated people. None of them wanted to leave Snow White with this girl.

They knew they would have to come up with some good Pony Pal ideas of how to save Snow White from Rema. They also knew that they didn't have time to have a private meeting. Something had to be done now.

Pam stepped forward. "Rema," she said, "Snow White might try to run away again. That could be dangerous because of cars and everything."

Anna added her idea. "Maybe Snow White should stay in the paddock with Acorn at night. That way you'll know she's safe."

Now it was Lulu's turn. "I could pick Snow White up here around six at night and bring her back first thing in the morning. I could take care of her for you, too. I'd even do stuff like wash out her water bucket and clean up the paddock."

"And when Lulu moves away, Anna and I could do all those things," Pam added.

Rema laughed right in their faces. "I can take care of my own horse, thank you very much," she said. "I might as well. There isn't anything else to do around here. And don't worry about Snow White. She won't be getting out at night anymore. I'm going to keep her in the stable most of the time."

Lulu's heart sank. She knew that Snow White was just like her. They both wanted to be outside as much as possible. Now Snow White was going to be locked up in a stable. Poor Snow White.

5

The Surprise

That night the Pony Pals were having their last barn sleepover.

As Lulu ate dinner with her grandmother, she was remembering all the great sleepovers she'd had with her friends. The girls would sleep in the barn while their ponies stayed out all night in the paddock. But tonight, while Acorn and Lightning were in the big Crandal paddock, Snow White would be alone in a cramped, hot stable.

Her grandmother interrupted Lulu's unhappy thoughts by saying, "I'll drive you to the Crandals', dear. But first I want to trim those bangs of yours. A hairdresser's grandaughter with straggly bangs just won't do."

Lulu was so depressed about Snow White that she didn't care what her grandmother did to her hair. She even let her give her a few curls.

"I'll miss you," Grandmother said as she fancied up Lulu's hair. "It's been wonderful having my granddaughter here. I'll even miss looking out the window and seeing that pretty pony of yours."

"Snow White's not my pony, Grandma," Lulu said sadly. "She's Rema Baxter's pony."

When Lulu got to Pam's house, she went directly to the paddocks and barn. But Anna and Pam weren't there. They must be in the kitchen, Lulu thought. She ran across the yard toward the house.

But there was no one in the kitchen except Woolie, the Crandals' dog.

"Anybody home?" Lulu called out.

"In here," Pam called back. "In the living room."

As Lulu and Woolie walked down the short hall to the living room, Lulu noticed that the house was strangely quiet. She pushed the living room door open. But no one was there.

"Pam?" Lulu said nervously. "Where are you?"

Suddenly people were coming at Lulu from *everywhere.*

The twins jumped out of their big toy box.

Dr. and Mrs. Crandal stepped out of a closet.

Anna's entire family rose up from behind the couch.

Grandmother Sanders, Pam, and the Pony Pals' friend, Ms. Wiggins, popped out from behind the drapes.

"SURPRISE!"

Everyone was yelling and laughing. Woolie was barking and jumping around.

Lulu was speechless. A surprise party just for her! It was the most wonderful surprise she'd ever had.

The dining room was decorated with periwinkle-blue streamers and balloons. "All the decorations are the Pony Pal color," Anna said, beaming.

"It's perfect," Lulu said.

In the middle of the table there was a huge brownie baked in the shape of a horseshoe. "For good luck," Anna's mother told Lulu.

Jill stood on a chair to put a wreath of daisies on Lulu's head. Jack had made a wreath, too. His was made of straw. "Because you love horses so much," he told her as he placed his wreath on top of Jill's.

And there were other presents. Ms. Wiggins gave Lulu a blank book with a red-plaid cloth cover. "It's for keeping a journal," she told Lulu. "You and your father live in such interesting places you really should keep a journal." Pam and her parents gave her a book called *The Ultimate Horse Book,* by Elwyn Hartley Edwards. Grandmother gave Lulu a fancy hairbrush-and-comb set. And Anna gave her a portrait she'd painted of Snow White!

Later, after the party was over, the Pony Pals went out to the paddock to say good night to Acorn and Lightning. Then they went into the barn and crawled into their sleeping bags.

"Thank you for the party," Lulu said. "It was the best."

"We thought of inviting Rema," Pam said.

"And then we met her," Anna added.

"Poor Snow White," they said in unison.

They were all silent for a few seconds, thinking about how Snow White was missing their last sleepover.

"I liked living in Wiggins," Lulu said. "Maybe Rema will like it, too. Maybe then she'll be a nicer person."

"I doubt it," Anna grumbled.

"I wonder where you'll live next, Lulu," Pam said.

"Wherever it is," Anna added, "I hope you'll like it as much as Wiggins."

"No place can be as good as Wiggins," Lulu said. "Because no place else will have the Pony Pals."

"I know what you mean," said Anna. "How could it?"

Pam and Lulu laughed.

"Did that sound conceited?" Anna asked.

"No," Lulu answered. "It sounded true. No one can replace you guys."

They fell asleep talking about all the Pony Pal adventures they'd had together.

Lulu dreamt about Snow White. In the dream she heard the pony crash against the side of a stall. The noise was so loud that the crash woke her up. But the noise wasn't a dream. It was *real*. Lulu knew there weren't any horses in the barn that night. But someone — or *something* — was in the barn. Anna reached over and grabbed Lulu's arm. The noise woke her up, too. Without saying a word, they woke up Pam. All three of them heard a loud grunt.

Lulu grabbed her flashlight. Without making a sound, the three girls wiggled out of their sleeping bags. The Pony Pals were going to find out whoever — or whatever — was in the barn.

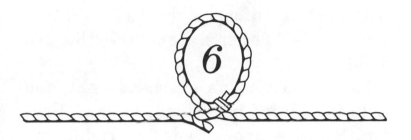

Bears!

What horrible, grunting creature was in
the barn? The Pony Pals tiptoed out of the
stall into the corridor. The barn was so dark
they couldn't even see one another. Then
Lulu pointed her flashlight into the black-
ness and turned the light on. In the beam
of yellow light the Pony Pals saw the back
of a huge . . . man.

They screamed.

The man screamed, too. He turned
around to face them.

"HELP!" Pam and Anna yelled.

"Dad!" Lulu yelled. "Oh, Daddy, it's you. It's you." She dropped the flashlight and ran into her father's arms. They hugged and kissed.

Pam turned on an overhead light, and Lulu introduced her friends to her father. Mr. Sanders apologized for frightening them and explained that in the dark he had tripped over a wooden stool. "I forgot to bring a flashlight," he explained.

"You made such a weird noise when you fell," Pam said.

"Like this?" Mr. Sanders asked. He grunted again. The girls laughed. "Hey," Mr. Sanders said, "it's about time for the sun to rise. Let's watch together."

Pam said the hayloft was the best place to watch the sunrise. The Pony Pals and Mr. Sanders sat on bales of hay and faced the east through the hayloft window.

"Dad, I thought you weren't coming home until Tuesday," Lulu said.

"I made better plane connections than I expected," he told her. "When I got to your grandmother's, she told me you were here. I came right over. I figured I'd surprise you."

"You sure did!" the Pony Pals said in unison.

Lulu's father put his arm around her and pulled her close. "I just couldn't wait to see you."

"Me either," Lulu said. "I have so much to tell you."

The girls told Lulu's father about the surprise party. Then they talked about their ponies, especially Snow White. "I wish I still had Snow White so I could introduce you," Lulu said. "You just missed her." Then Lulu told her dad about giving Snow White back to Rema.

When the bottom curve of the sun had cleared Mount Morris, Lulu looked over to her dad. He had a little smile on his face and was staring at her. "Why are you looking at me like that?" she asked.

"I'm amazed at you," he said. "You've grown up so much in these past months.

You seem so independent and . . . responsible."

"That's because of Snow White," Lulu said. "I learned a lot from taking care of her." She looked over at Anna and Pam. "And I learned a lot from being a Pony Pal."

"We have Pony Pal Power," Anna explained. "When we work together on a problem, we can usually find a solution."

"Even when grown-ups can't," Pam added.

Now that the sun was up, they all went out to the paddock to introduce Mr. Sanders to Acorn and Lightning. They even showed him where Pony Pal Trail began at the edge of the paddock.

When Lulu and her father got into the car to go back to Grandmother Sanders', Lulu leaned out the car window and told her friends, "Go for a trail ride today and have fun. Don't worry about me. I have to pack and stuff. I'll see you before I leave town."

As they were driving along, Lulu asked

her father, "Where are we going to live next, Dad?"

Her father smiled at her but didn't answer.

"Come on, Dad. Where?"

"Lulu," her father began. "I missed you like crazy when I was working in the Amazon. And I know that you missed me. But I also know how happy you've been here in Wiggins."

"Dad, you're not going to leave me here and go away without me again. Please, Dad," Lulu pleaded. "I missed you so much."

"Let me finish," he said. "I've figured out a project for around here. I wrote a proposal." He looked over at Lulu again. "And I found out yesterday I got a grant to do it. For now, we'll both be living in Wiggins!"

"What animal will you study, Dad?" Lulu asked. "I bet it's the whitetail deer."

"Nope," he said. "I'm doing a research project on the black bear. They've been coming back to this region."

"Bears!" Lulu exclaimed. She couldn't wait to tell Pam and Anna. "That's neat, Dad. Can I help you?"

"Sure," he said. "Just like always."

Lulu smiled at her dad as they pulled into the driveway. She loved living in Wiggins. She was happy that she could stay with Pam and Anna, and be with her dad. But Lulu's smile disappeared when she thought of Snow White.

"What's wrong, Lulu?" her father asked. "I thought you'd be glad."

"I am," Lulu said. "I really am." Lulu tried to smile again. But it was hard. How could she live in Wiggins without Snow White?

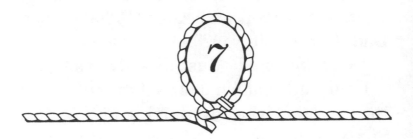

Not a Very Good Rider

After breakfast, Lulu's father went upstairs to take a nap. "He's exhausted from his long trip," her grandmother said. "He'll sleep all day."

The front doorbell rang. Grandmother's first client of the day had arrived. She'd be busy in her beauty parlor until dinnertime.

Lulu telephoned Pam's house. She wanted to tell Anna and Pam that she wasn't moving after all. Mrs. Crandal answered and told Lulu that the girls had already left for a day of trail riding on the Wiggins estate.

After Lulu did the breakfast dishes, she sat at the kitchen table. Now what would she do? If Snow White was still *her* pony, Lulu thought, she could go for a ride. Instead, Lulu sadly put on her hiking boots. She would go for a hike.

Lulu walked on Main Street until she reached Mudge Road. Then on Mudge Road she made a right onto Lilac Lane. Lulu was headed for the Baxters' paddock.

Lulu wasn't going to visit with Snow White. She knew that Snow White needed time to adjust to being with Rema again. But Lulu just had to check that Rema was letting Snow White out in the paddock during the day.

When she got close to the Baxter property, Lulu walked behind bushes on the other side of the road. She didn't want Snow White to see her. But there was no pony to hide from. Snow White wasn't in the paddock. Lulu checked carefully. No Snow White.

Was Rema keeping Snow White locked up in the stable all day long, too? How horrible! Lulu was feeling angry and trying to decide what to do next when she heard horses' hooves pounding on the dirt road.

She saw Rema trotting Snow White around a bend in Lilac Lane. But Rema's body wasn't in rhythm with Snow White's trot. Lulu wanted to call out, "Put your legs back!" She knew that if Rema corrected her seat, she and Snow White would both be more comfortable. Suddenly, Rema halted Snow White with a strong tug on the rein. The sides of Lulu's mouth ached in sympathy for the pony.

Rema leaned over the side of her saddle to adjust her stirrup. Then she moved Snow White back into a trot. But she still wasn't posting correctly. Lulu could see that Rema wasn't having a good time. And neither was Snow White.

"I don't know what's wrong with you,

Snow White," Rema said. "I shouldn't have let that kid take care of you. She ruined you for sure."

Lulu wanted to jump out from hiding to tell Rema, "That's not true. *You're* the one who doesn't know how to ride Snow White." But arguing with Rema wouldn't help anything. And shouting would only upset Snow White. Lulu decided to get out of there before she was discovered. She wanted to find her Pony Pals.

She turned to the dense woods behind her. There was a deer-run tunnel through the underbrush. She walked through it until the tunnel opened into a big square field where a dozen or so whitetail deer were grazing. Lulu moved silently around the edge of the field. One of the deer looked up and saw her. The deer let out a high-pitched warning shriek that sent the herd leaping into the woods.

By the time Lulu came to a road, she was hot and thirsty. But she didn't care. She needed to find the quickest way to the Wiggins estate. She needed to find Pam and Anna.

Lulu imagined her map of Wiggins. She was on Mudge Road Extension. Badd Brook ran parallel to Mudge Road. Following Badd Brook would be a perfect shortcut into the Wiggins estate.

Lulu had been walking along the brook for half an hour when she heard Acorn's familiar nicker. Just then Pam and Anna rode their ponies around a turn in the trail. Lulu noticed how sad her friends looked.

Pam was the first to see Lulu. Her sad look exploded into a big grin. "Look who's here," she told Anna.

"Lulu!" Anna screamed. "It's Lulu."

Lulu loved how happy her friends were to see her. They dismounted and led their ponies on foot so they could walk with Lulu. "Why did you guys look so miserable before?" Lulu asked. "What's wrong?"

"We were already missing you," Anna said.

"Well, forget that," Lulu told them. "Because I'm not moving after all. My dad's going to work on a project right here in Wiggins."

The Pony Pals yelled "Yes!" and hit high fives. Acorn and Lightning neighed, as if they understood the good news.

"And guess what else?" Lulu said.

"What?" Anna and Pam asked in unison.

"My dad's going to be studying black bears. They're coming back to this area. He's going to write an article about them for *National Geographic*."

"Bears!" Pam said.

"Great!" said Anna.

They did another round of high fives.

"And he said we could help him," Lulu added.

They did so many high fives that the palms of their hands stung.

"But I have some bad news, too," Lulu said. "Which is mainly why I came looking for you."

She told the other Pony Pals how she

spied on Rema and Snow White and that Rema was a terrible rider.

"I'm not surprised," Anna said.

"How did she win all those ribbons we saw hanging in the stable?" Lulu wondered out loud.

"Maybe she *was* a good rider," Pam said. "But she hasn't ridden in a long time. She must have forgotten a lot."

"She blames me for her bad riding," Lulu said. "I heard her tell Snow White."

"That's just like Rema to blame someone else for her problems," Anna said.

For once Pam and Lulu totally agreed with Anna's opinion of Rema.

"Lulu, you're the one who should be riding Snow White," Pam said.

"If you're going to be living in Wiggins, you should have her," Anna said.

"But how?" Lulu asked.

"We'll each come up with an idea of how you can get Snow White back," Pam said.

"Let's meet at the diner at seven o'clock

to put our ideas together," Anna suggested.

"Don't worry, Lulu," Pam said. "We'll come up with a Pony Pal plan for getting Snow White back."

"Remember, we have Pony Pal Power," Anna added.

The Pony Pals went to the field they liked best for jumping stone walls. Lulu took turns jumping Acorn and Lightning. But three girls with two ponies just wasn't the same as three girls with three ponies.

Lulu walked home along Pony Pal Trail beside her friends and their ponies. She missed Snow White so badly that tears came to her eyes. What if she couldn't get Snow White back?

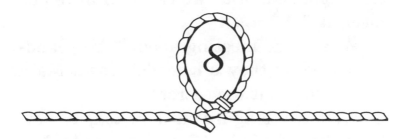

Three Good Ideas

After dinner, Lulu asked her grandmother and father if she could go over to Off-Main Diner with her friends.

"What would you think of me coming along with you?" her father asked. "I'd like to meet some of my new neighbors."

"That'd be great," Lulu answered. "It's a very popular diner. Anna's mother owns it. We'll introduce you to lots of people."

Pam and Anna were waiting for Lulu on Anna's front porch. "My dad's coming, too," she explained. "But we can still have our meeting."

"What's the meeting about?" Mr. Sanders asked as they all headed down Main Street. "Or is it top secret?"

"We have to figure out how to get Snow White back for Lulu," Pam explained to Mr. Sanders.

"Lulu needs a pony," Anna added.

"My goodness," Mr. Sanders said, "of course she does. I've been so jet-lagged I haven't been thinking clearly. Wiggins is a great place to have a pony. Could Lulu still keep a pony in your paddock, Anna?"

"Sure," Anna answered.

"It's settled then," Mr. Sanders said. "We'll get you a pony, Lulu. That'll be terrific."

Anna and Pam cheered. And Lulu acted excited and thanked her dad. But she was thinking that the only pony for her was Snow White.

"I should introduce my father to some people before we have our meeting," Lulu whispered to Anna and Pam, "so he won't be alone."

"There's someone he should meet," Anna said as they walked into the diner. She was pointing to the counter where Ms. Wiggins was eating her dinner.

All the Pony Pals were friends with Ms. Wiggins. But Anna was closest to her because they were both dyslexic and they were both artists. Also, they both had Shetland ponies.

Ms. Wiggins looked up and saw the Pony Pals. "Hi, girls," she said. She looked right at Mr. Sanders and added, "I'll bet you're Lulu's father. You look so much alike."

"Why, thank you," Mr. Sanders said. He put an arm around Lulu's shoulder. "I consider that a huge compliment."

"As well you should," Ms. Wiggins said. She put out her hand.

Mr. Sanders smiled as he shook Ms. Wiggins' hand and said, "I'm Tom Sanders."

"I'm Winifred Wiggins. I'm glad to meet you, Tom. But I'm not glad you'll be taking Lulu away. We're all going to miss her."

"No, we're not," Anna said.

"We're not?" Ms. Wiggins asked with surprise.

"Nope," Anna said. "Because Lulu's not moving!"

They all laughed. Then Mr. Sanders told Ms. Wiggins that he was going to live in Wiggins for awhile.

"He's going to study black bears," Lulu explained. "And write an article about them."

Soon Ms. Wiggins and Mr. Sanders were sitting next to one another at the counter. She was telling him all about a black bear that she'd sighted on the Wiggins estate.

The Pony Pals made themselves ice-cream sodas and brought them to the back booth. It was time to go over their ideas for how to get Snow White back.

"It's great that your father said he'd buy you a pony, Lulu," Pam said.

"I'd rather *rent* Snow White than *buy* an-

other pony," Lulu said. "That's what my idea's about."

Lulu handed Pam a slip of paper. She read it aloud.

Lease Snow White from Rema.
Tell her she can still ride Snow
White whenever she wants.

"That way Rema can make some money and still ride," Lulu explained. "You can tell by the way she dresses that she likes to buy things. And, if she wants, I'll do all the stable chores."

"Rema must really hate mucking out," Anna commented.

"Lulu, I like your idea," Pam said. "If it works we should also try to get her to take some riding lessons. It sounds like she needs them."

"I'm not sure that she should be riding Snow White at all," Anna said. "That's what *my* idea is about." Anna put a drawing in the middle of the table.

Lulu and Pam laughed at the picture. "You got her perfect," Pam said. "You could draw cartoons for the newspaper."

"Rema's not *that* big," Lulu said.

"But I bet you anything she's too big for Snow White," Anna said. "She's taller than any of us. I bet that's why she has trouble riding."

"Why didn't I think of that?" Pam wondered out loud. "You're right, Anna. And it fits right in with *my* idea."

Pam gave her idea to Lulu to read out loud.

Get Rema to buy a horse so she'll sell Snow White to Lulu.

"Remember how she kept calling Snow White a horse instead of a pony?" Pam asked. "She thinks she's too grown-up for a pony. So she should get a horse. A big one. Then you can buy Snow White, Lulu."

"Olson's horse farm has tons of horses," Anna said. "Mr. Olson would have a good horse for Rema. Something like that black Morgan he tried to sell me would be perfect for her."

"We've got a lot to tell Rema," Lulu said. "But how are we going to get her to listen to us? She thinks we're just these little kids who don't know anything."

"Leave it to me," Pam said. "I'll call her up and *schedule* a *business meeting*. She loves that sort of thing."

"You're the best one to do it," Anna said to Pam.

Lulu agreed.

"What'll you say if she asks you what the meeting is about?" Anna asked.

"I'll tell her that it's too important to discuss on the phone," Pam answered.

"Rema will love that, too," said Anna.

Pam got up and went to the pay phone near the kitchen. In a few minutes she came back. "We're meeting at her place at ten o'clock tomorrow morning," Pam told them proudly.

The Pony Pals were glad. But they didn't hit high fives. They all knew that getting Rema Baxter to sell Snow White would be one of the toughest challenges the Pony Pals ever faced.

You Shrunk My Pony

The next morning the Pony Pals met on the town green. They were wearing their best clothes for the meeting with Rema Baxter.

As they walked along Lilac Lane toward the Baxters' property, they saw that Snow White wasn't in her paddock. "I told you, Rema locks her up during the day," Lulu said to the others.

By the time they rang the doorbell, the Pony Pals were more determined than ever to get Snow White back.

Rema let them in. "Good morning," she said. "Follow me." She led them down a hall and into the dining room.

Rema sat at the head of the table. She instructed Pam to sit to her right. Anna and Lulu were to sit on her left.

Before Pam could say why they were there, Rema said, "Lucinda Sanders, you have damaged my horse."

The Pony Pals were so surprised by what Rema said that for a second they were speechless.

Finally, Lulu said, "What are you talking about?"

"Lulu took the best care of Snow White," Pam said.

"She even saved her life!" Anna added.

"Is Snow White sick?" Lulu asked Rema in a hushed, frightened voice.

"If she's sick," Anna told Rema, "it's because you keep her locked up all the time."

"What are her symptoms?" Pam asked. "My father's a veterinarian. We can get him over here right away."

"My first complaint," Rema said, "is that you didn't feed her enough. She's lost weight so she's smaller than she used to be."

"Lulu fed Snow White plenty," Anna said. "Snow White didn't shrink."

"Don't interrupt," Rema scolded. "My second complaint is that Lucinda Sanders ruined Snow White's fine schooling. Snow White used to be an excellent ride. She doesn't work the same way since Lucinda rode her."

Pam stood up and spoke in a commanding voice. "Now it's our turn to talk, Rema Baxter. First of all, Snow White didn't lose weight. You are too tall for Snow White now, so she seems smaller to you."

"How much did you grow when you were away at school this year?" Anna asked.

"Two inches," Rema boasted.

"You were probably already too big for Snow White when you left for school. Now you're way too big," Pam told her.

"If you're not the right size for a pony,"

Lulu explained, "it doesn't feel right when you ride. It's uncomfortable for the pony, too."

"Why don't you sell Snow White and buy a horse that's the right size for you," Pam advised.

Rema tapped a pencil eraser on the table. She was deep in thought. The Pony Pals didn't say a word. They all had their fingers crossed under the table.

Finally, Rema broke the silence by wondering out loud, "But if I got a horse, what would I do with it when I went back to school?"

"Maybe you don't want a horse anymore," Pam suggested.

"I bet there's something else you'd like to do with the money you make by selling Snow White," Anna said. "Something you want very badly."

"There is," Rema exclaimed. "If I could make some quick money I could go to sleepaway camp this summer with my boarding school friends. Then I woudn't have to stay in boring Wiggins."

The Pony Pals smiled and nodded at Rema.

"Great idea," Anna said. "Sleep-away camp is so much fun." Anna winked at Lulu.

"I'd like to buy Snow White," Lulu told Rema.

"Okay," Rema said. "I'll sell you Snow White. But not for a penny less than . . . two thousand dollars."

The Pony Pals couldn't believe their ears. Lulu knew that her father wouldn't — couldn't — spend that much on a pony.

"You just made that number up," Anna said. "You don't know how much Snow White is worth."

"You need an expert to price a pony," Lulu said. "Like Mr. Olson."

"Mr. Olson buys and sells horses and ponies all the time," Pam explained to Rema. "He'd help you decide how much to charge for Snow White."

"All right," Rema said. "I'll talk to this Mr. Olson. I'll call him right now."

As Rema looked up Olson's phone number in the phone book, the Pony Pals exchanged little smiles. Mr. Olson would set a fair price. It still wasn't time for high fives, but at least there was a chance that Lulu could get Snow White back.

"Hello, Mr. Olson," Rema said into the phone. "I'm Rema Baxter and I have a prize pony to sell. She's a very special eight-year-old Welsh pony, thirteen-point-two hands high. She's very beautiful. I was wondering if you had any clients that might be interested."

Lulu waved her hand in front of Rema's face. "*I'm* interested. *I'm* the one who wants to buy Snow White."

Rema scowled at Lulu and continued her conversation with Mr. Olson.

When Rema hung up the phone, Lulu repeated, "I said I wanted to buy Snow White."

"I realize that, Lucinda," Rema said.

"But you're not the only one who might like to buy Snow White."

"But I took care of her," Lulu said.

"We're the ones who came up with the idea of selling her in the first place," Pam put in.

"You're not being fair," Anna complained.

"Lucinda, if you want to buy Snow White," Rema said, "come to Mr. Olson's farm at three o'clock. There'll be other people there who will be interested in buying her."

Rema led them to the door. "Thank you for coming by," she said. "I think we had a very productive meeting."

Sold!

Lulu's father was in the kitchen when Lulu got home. He looked rested and was eating a huge breakfast.

"Well, good morning," he said with a smile and wide-open arms.

Lulu gave her father a big hug. It was so wonderful to have him back. She sat on his knee and told him the news that Snow White was for sale.

"Perfect," her father said. "That's the pony we'll get. But I hope she's not a prize pony with fancy papers. We only have so much money we can spend for a pony."

Lulu wished she and Snow White hadn't won all those ribbons in the horse shows. She hoped that Snow White wasn't such a special pony, after all.

At two-thirty Lulu and her dad hiked over to Mr. Olson's. They were near the end of the shortcut trail between Off-Main Diner and the horse farm when Lulu heard the clippity-clop of horses behind them. Anna and Pam were riding their ponies over to Olson's to help Lulu buy Snow White.

When they came out at Olson's farm, Lulu saw Mr. Baxter's station wagon. There was another, very expensive car parked right next to the Baxters' car. Lulu guessed that anybody who had a car that fancy could afford an expensive prize pony.

"I know that car," Anna said.

"Whose is it?" Pam asked.

"Tommy Rand's mother's!" Anna answered.

The Pony Pals gasped. Tommy Rand was a mean, bossy kid in the eighth grade. He'd rented Acorn when he was in the fourth grade. The Pony Pals thought that Acorn must have had a terrible life with a kid like Tommy Rand. Did Tommy Rand want to buy Snow White?

"Tommy wouldn't want a pony," Pam said. "All he cares about is football and teasing girls."

"But his sister might," Anna said. "Look!"

They saw Mr. Olson leading Snow White around the side of the barn. With him were Tommy Rand, his sister Anita, Mrs. Rand, the Baxters, and Rema.

Pam and Anna dismounted their ponies and walked with Lulu and her father to the group gathered around Snow White.

"Hi, girls," Mr. Olson said cheerfully. "What can I do for you today?" He winked at Anna. "Ready to trade Acorn for my beautiful black Morgan?"

"You know I wouldn't give up Acorn," Anna told him.

"Well, look who's here. It's the Pony Pests," Tommy Rand said.

Anita ignored her brother and said a friendly hi to Pam, Anna, and Lulu. They knew Anita Rand from school and thought she was nice. They felt sorry for her because she had Tommy Rand for a brother.

Lulu gave Snow White a hello rub on the neck. She looked into the pony's eyes to tell her that she missed her and was trying to get her back. Snow White gently nudged Lulu's shoulder.

"I guess you girls came to say good-bye to Snow White." Mr. Olson patted Snow White on the shoulder. "She's a nice pony," he said. "A real winner."

"I'm here to *buy* Snow White," Lulu said.

"But I just bought her," Anita told Lulu.

"Anita rode her and liked her very much," Mrs. Rand explained. "And we've agreed to the price."

Lulu glared at Rema. "You said to come at three o'clock."

"Did I?" Rema said with a smile. "Well, I suppose you could bid on Snow White since you're here now. We could have a little auction."

"Why is anyone talking to these pests?" Tommy Rand asked. Lulu noticed that his mother just ignored him. So did the Pony Pals.

Mr. Olson was surprised by Rema's suggestion that they have a horse auction. "That's not how we work these things," Mr. Olson told her. "You asked me to suggest a price. I did. You accepted it. The Rands said they're willing to pay the amount."

Mrs. Baxter shot Rema an angry look. "Why didn't you tell me that the girl who saved Snow White's life wanted to buy her?" Mrs. Baxter asked Rema.

"Mom," Rema hissed. "We can make more money this way. It's good business."

"No, it's not," Mrs. Baxter said.

While Mrs. Baxter and Rema were talk-

372

ing, the Pony Pals were thinking. They needed three ideas — quick. This was their last chance to get Snow White back.

"I took care of Snow White while Rema was away at school," Lulu told Anita. "Snow White is a wonderful pony. I'm sure you'll love her. How long will you be trying her out?"

"Most people try a pony at least a week before the purchase is final," Pam said. "Isn't that right, Mr. Olson?"

"I insist on it," Mr. Olson said. "Unless they've leased the animal first. The Rands understand how it's done. A small deposit. A week's trial."

"And a veterinarian checkup to be sure Snow White is in perfect health," Pam added.

"Then," Mr. Olson continued, "we collect the rest of the money and the sale is final."

"Wait a minute," Rema said. "You mean I won't get all my money today?"

"That's how this business is done, young lady," her father said sternly.

Anna gave Acorn's reins to Pam and went over to the paddock where the black Morgan was grazing. "Look at this beautiful horse, Anita," she said. "Isn't he wonderful?"

"Oh, that Morgan is a beauty," Lulu said.

"I didn't see him before," Anita commented as she moved toward the paddock. The Morgan came over to the girls at the fence.

"I could see you on that Morgan, Anita," Pam said. "He's a little bigger than Snow White. But looking at your height and the Morgan's size, I'd say he's perfect for you."

Anita was hardly listening. She was looking deep into the eyes of the Morgan and rubbing his cheek.

"If you'd like, I could saddle him up so you could give him a try," Mr. Olson told Anita.

"Please," Anita said. "If it's not too late, I'd like to try him, too."

Mr. Baxter and Tommy Rand grumbled

and complained about the wait. Everyone else — except Rema — agreed that Anita should try the Morgan. When he was saddled up, Anita mounted and rode him around the ring a few times.

After her ride, Anita pulled him up alongside the paddock fence where everyone was waiting and watching. Mr. Olson told Anita, "Now that I've seen you ride both Snow White and the Morgan, I'd say the Morgan suits you better. What do you think?"

"I want the Morgan," Anita said. Then she cantered the horse around the ring again.

"Oh, great," Tommy Rand said. "Just great. We'll never get out of here."

"This isn't fair," Rema grumbled. "She already said she wanted Snow White."

Meanwhile, Lulu and her father exchanged a glance. Sometimes they understood one another without talking — just like the Pony Pals. "Mr. Baxter," said Mr.

Sanders, "I was wondering if you would tell me what price has been set for Snow White?"

Mr. Baxter whispered a figure in Mr. Sanders' ear. Lulu's father gave her the thumbs-up sign.

"Mr. Baxter," Lulu said, "if Anita would like to buy the Morgan, I would like to buy Snow White. I don't need a week to try her because I took care of her for a long time. We could finalize the sale right now."

"You mean I could get all the money today?" Rema said. "And go to camp?"

"The sooner the better," Anna mumbled.

"If the Sanders girl would like Snow White," Mrs. Rand said, "we would be happy to shift our deposit onto the Morgan."

Anita had dismounted. She laid her head on the Morgan's neck. "I already love him," she said. "And I don't even know his name. What is it?"

"Morgan," Mr. Olson and the Pony Pals answered in unison. Everyone laughed.

"What do you say, Mr. Baxter?" Mr. Olson asked.

"It's okay with me," Mr. Baxter said.

"Me too!" Rema exclaimed.

"So let's do some business here," Mr. Olson said. "Anita Rand takes Morgan on trial. And Lulu Sanders buys Snow White."

The Pony Pals shouted "Yes!" and hit high fives and danced around. Then Lulu gave Snow White a great big hug and kiss.

Snow White neighed, as if to say, "Can we go home now, Lulu?"